COLE MACHIA

# UP, DOWN,

# DOWN,

# ANYWAY

Up, Down, Down, Anyway

Copyright © 2014 by Cole Machia

Published by Vraidex

First printing 2014

Printed in the United States of America

# CHAPTER *1*

I WAS BORN the day after Elvis died. My mamma said I came out early, by a couple weeks, I guess, like a whatchacallit, a premie or something. She said it felt like I was comin out sideways I hurt her so bad. But I don't remember any of that shit. What I do remember, and it's one of my earliest memories, is hearing the Elvis Christmas album. It was Christmas time, and my momma told me she sometimes wondered if I wasn't Elvis back from the dead, reincarnated or something, and maybe that's why I came out so early. This was Christmas time, man. I was just barely getting around the whole Jesus Christ coming back from the dead thing, and she went and threw that out at me. Well, hell, you know, I think that did something to me, man. I really do.

So…

I play *Love Me* at the beginning. Every time. Just about every night. It's been that way for, I don't know, ten years. I don't know what put me to it, and I can't think of ever really bothering about it, but I've always known better than to start a show with anything really popular. You start out with something too well known, something they've heard over and over already, you're just handing them their excuse to move on. If they've heard it before, they don't need to hear it again. Especially from no pretender. I like to get at least one good song through to them. And *Love Me* does the trick every time.

I guess 'cause it's a slow starter, that song. And it don't really speed up none, but it builds, and by the time I get to the end of the song people think I've done something with it, and they seem to like me for it. But I've never changed a thing. I do it just the way he did it. I do it right. I don't change a single thing. Not one note. *Baby what you want me to do* goes in the middle, every time. And, every time, almost every night, *It's now or never* wraps it up. Ends it nice and loud. Nice and big. The rest of the show I just throw around random, whatever I feel like playing that night; but every show has to have the same beginning, middle and end. It almost always works. A lot of folks have questioned me for ending with *It's now or never*, but I'll tell you… even most people that hate that song will tell you it's the best crescendo the King ever had. The best. Cause I don't really account for the gospel ones.

I been doing the same show so long, my life kinda got wrapped up inside of it. Been doing it longer than almost anything. Almost longer than all my school years, even. It's gotten to the point I can't see my life any other way. My whole personal history is chopped up, centered on those three songs like… like old pictures. --Like those old pictures of people from the early nineteen hundreds. You just kind of picture them always standing the way they stand in the photographs, always squinting the way they're squinting, their lips pursed out or drawn tight... hardly ever a smile. That's how you always see them, so that's how they always were. They never walked to where they were going, never scratched an itch or actually gave birth to no children, not in the breaking water sense and burying afterbirth- or slipping it in the soup broth- depending on custom. That's how I saw myself, I guess. Kind of fixed. Kind of hazy and sepia toned. That's that beginning, middle, and end for you, and who really cares about the rest of the show.

The owner of the place still lets people smoke inside. Something about the law only applying to individuals. A cop will only make a stink if they actually see you smoking. They have to see you with a cigarette in your hand, with their own eyes, if they want to cite you. Other than that, it's all ignorance, and a three foot cloud of smoke hovering over the bar apparently don't mean a thing. I lighted a cigarette while the band packed up their equipment. I only had my one acoustic and had carried it over to the bar with me, setting it next to the stool without even bothering with a guitar case. I wanted a snakeskin case, hadn't yet found a cheap one, and so hadn't got any kind. You know how it is.

The three people I considered the audience (cause they sat at the tables instead of the bar) clapped hollowly, and the eight people sitting at the bar ignored me, looked down at their drinks. I cleared my throat sort of loud, I guess to get the attention of at least one of 'em, took a drag from the cigarette and exhaled loudly, but it made no difference.

*You believe this shit?*

People got a right not to be entertained, though, I suppose. You can't fault 'em none if they don't have no enthusiasm. I just hope I never get to be that way, man. I took another drag, held my cigarette sheepishly close to the communal beer can ashtray, just in case, and smiled a little. A little judgmentally. Kind of high on myself.

"Headed to Pico's if you want to follow along," fella named Roy said, slapping me on the back, indicating the rest of the band as they flowed outside single file. Roy played stand-up base, and he played it damn good, too. But they was the house band and it didn't do no good to fraternize outside work. Didn't do me no good, anyway.

"I just might, Roy. Thank you. In about fifteen, though. Let me get a beer down first."

Roy shot a thumbs up and made a sort of click-click noise in his cheek, but I don't think he really paid no attention to my response. Seemed he was out the door with the rest of the band before my complimentary beer came. I was wondering who the three note asshole thought he was trying to kid when some girl slid into the stool beside me. The bruised up knees on her finely sculpted legs brushed up against my guitar, and of course I noticed that first.

"You play some good Elvis," she said. I thought with a sort of purr. "Kind of refreshing, almost."

"Uh- thank you, ma'am. I really app... I appreciate

that."

"It's weird to see anyone do it like you anymore. Without the collar and the cape. All those guys make it seem almost a joke. But you sound real good. But I guess if you didn't do it so good--" *Damn, she's a pretty one.* "--people wouldn't know you was supposed to be him."

"Well, I don't think, um, that I'm doing it to be him, really. I guess I'm more, just kind of doing it to be good, and he was… well, he was really the only good one."

*Damn pretty! Come on, baby. Baby, you're so pretty my hands are sweating.*

"My daddy had Elvis on the record player all the time. Been a long time since I thought of home," she said. I think with a purr. "You made me feel kind of comfortable, you know, with your singing. Kinda like home."

*Come on, sweetheart.*

*Say it, man. Come on. Say it!*

*Baby you're so fine. If your face was on a dog, I'd be fuckin dogs. I'd be a dog fucker right now, baby.*

"Well, I appreciate that, ma'am. I'm really glad you liked it." I drank my beer down in three gulps and wiped my mouth with the back of my hand. "It's really nice."

She stared at me for a few seconds. Her eyes narrowed. Smoky green eyes. My Adam's apple throbbed and I looked at myself in the mirror behind the bar. Then she tapped my guitar with her sharp red nails and moved one stool over and away from me. I heard her order another drink. My mood started to sour and I hesitated to get up. I kind of wanted another beer, but the house only swung for one. When the first one is free, five bucks seems an awful lot for the second. And then you gotta tip. I didn't tip on the first one cause, well, cause it was a free drink, right? So I'd have to tip if I had a second. Really, if I ordered a second beer, I'd kind of have to tip double to cover for the first. That's how it works. I inhaled strongly and got the nasty hot box before pinching the filter into the can and exhaled quickly, sending the smoke long and straight toward the ceiling fan. My hand started to shake a little and I could feel my face forming a frown. And what was the band going to think when I didn't show up at Pico's? How was that going to look? I thought about going, but damn it, I really did not want to. Who the hell were they to make me feel guilty about not going somewhere I didn't want to go? And Pico's is horrible food. And the drinks are way overpriced. I could grab another couple beers where I was, though, and it'd be cheaper and I wouldn't be likely to order any of Pico's overpriced piss.

*She's still at the bar. She hasn't left! Shit.*

I leaned over to grab my guitar. By the time I rose back up, Mitch Connelly, the owner of the place was staring right up my nose.

"Come on back to the office, Frank," he said, turning to lead the way before I could say anything.

Mitch weighed two hundred and fifty pounds and had a Santa Claus beard, but he moved down the snaking corridor to his back office like he was skinny as me. I kept waiting for him to bump against the wall and set off a buzzer like in that Operation game, but he wore his weight too well for that. The door to his office was already open, and he waved me inside. He sort of twirled behind his desk, slumped into the chair and kicked his feet onto the desk in one graceful move. Like a god- danged ballerina.

"Got a problem," he said, beckoning for me to have a seat in one of the cold plastic chairs set against the wall. I sat.

"Watcha say, Mitch. What kind of problem?"

"Oh," he began, letting that first vowel swim on a long breath. "One button-down blue shirt and a black leather jacket for a starter. Catch my drift, Frank."

"Huh-uh. Not yet, anyway," I said, sneaking a peak at what I had on. A button-down blue shirt and a black leather jacket.

Mitch's chair creaked as he leaned back a bit. Then he swung his feet off the desk and planted them firmly on the ground. "It just ain't working anymore, Frank. If it ever did. This whole skinny Elvis thing. Well, it doesn't really count, does it? Ahhh--" he let that one swim too. "Customers come here expecting a show, Frank. And I'm afraid I can't say in all honesty that that's what we've been giving them."

"Well, I'm uh, I don't really agree, Mitch. I play a full set four days a week. An hour and a half set- almost a two hour set. Almost a two hour set of mostly two and a half, three minute songs, Mitch," I said. *You mother fucker.* "Mitch, I think that's a hell of a show."

Mitch leaned forward, looking kind of serious. "Come on, Frank," he said, quietly, almost confidingly. "Ain't no show with a three person crowd."

"I counted eleven."

"Only three at the tables, though, Frank. The bar ain't audience and you know it. And yes, I know three is about the worst it gets. We had fifteen the day before yesterday, but fifteen ain't a whole hell of a lot in a house that sits eighty seven. On your best day, your *best* day, there ain't no show with an audience of fifteen."

"Now, hold on a minute, Mitch--"

"When you were a kid playing for your brother and sisters, did you call that a show? When you're practicing in front of the mirror, you call that a show? There ain't no show here, Frank. It's like I'm paying you to practice. I feel like I'm paying you to practice. And it's not just you. It's Roy and Mike and Hopper, too. And they're under contract, Frank. I got to pay them no matter who they're backing." He pressed his thumbs into his beard under his chin, as if he needed them to hold his head up. "I can't help it, Frank. It ain't my doing. It ain't my fault that fifteen ain't no crowd. That's just the way it is. How it is anywhere. You can't fault me for that now, can you? Christ's sake."

"Aw, come on now, Mitch. I'm not faulting you for anything. I didn't say anything. It's just... well, you know, what do you want me to do about it?"

Mitch's head pivoted on his thumbs. "Gotta let you go, Frank-o," he said.

"Say what?"

"It don't work, Frank. I got to find another act. No

crowd means no business. If you can't bring in a crowd, you can't bring me any business and that's the whole point of you being here. Matter of fact, it kinda seems like you chase business away. It just don't make no sense for a cocktail lounge to have only three people during happy hour."

"You can't put that on me, Mitch. Almost every dang place within three miles is a cocktail lounge. They all got happy hours. That ain't my fault."

"They also got business…"

"Mitch…"

"And I'll tell you something else they got…"

"Now, listen…"

"A. Fat. Elvis. A big fat fucker Elvis. With the rhinestones and a damn cape and damn mutton chops down to here," he patted himself right above the crotch.

I didn't say anything.

"Hell, Frank. Most of 'em don't even sing. Most of 'em's just karee-o-kee-yin'. I could get me one of those guys for a hundred dollars a week. Get a cheap sound system and actually make a prophet for once."

I smiled kind of nervous. "Come on, Mitch. You don't want none of that stuff. That stuff costs money, too. Think about it. And what are you gonna do with the house band? How do you think they're gonna take this?"

"The band ain't the problem. It's you. You're the main act, but no one wants to see you. And I'm not trying to say you ain't no good. It ain't that. It's just… you ain't doing the shtick right. You got the music down pat, I mean it, but without the costume

9

you're just a half-ass. And nobody likes a half-ass. Hell, Frank, most people's half-asses already, they don't want to pay good money to see another one sing at 'em."

I felt queasy in my stomach. It was one of those moments you know arguing won't do you any good. When anything other than acceptance just makes you look stupider. There ain't ever really anything you can say when someone doesn't want you around.

"This is a bunch of bullshit," I said. "Mitch. Please. I'm begging you."

Yeah. I know.

"So that's it? No two weeks? No severance? Nothing."

He snorted. "Severance? Frank. Come on."

It got real quiet for a couple minutes. Then Mitch took a deep breath and flopped his hands down on his desk, and for some reason I jumped. Not very noticeable... but if he'd been looking. And I wondered all of a sudden if he didn't maybe want me to be a little scared. Like maybe he'd rather I hauled ass chicken shit from his office rather than beg for my job. Then I started to do the math. His two hundred and fifty pounds against my one fifty-five. I wondered how fast he could jump from around his desk, or if I was quick enough to surprise *him*... or if he might take a lunge at me while I was wondering if he would. They was messy thoughts.

Now you don't dedicate your life to impersonating the Tiger Man without knowing a little somethin'-somethin'. I'd taken Judo since junior high, and a little karat-ey. But I couldn't see myself trading punches with no full grown man. I'd sure thought about it a lot, but much as I thought about it, I never could imagine hitting somebody with enough force to put em down real quick. I imagined it kinda how it feels punching people in dreams; your brains don't know your hands ain't moving, so you never can punch hard enough. I sure wouldn't like to sock a man in the jaw and leave em ready to do the same to me. If I couldn't put em down with one good punch it was just better to leave it be, so far as I was concerned. So yeah, I suppose you could call me a sissy. Or at least something like that. So... I didn't swing at him, and he didn't swing at me, and I didn't have no damn job anymore.

The sun seemed extra bright when I stepped outside, and I squinted into it. I skid my boots over the gravel of the unpaved parking lot, leaving a trail all the way to my Caddy. I sighed deep, looking back at Mitch's place and felt a strange sense of loss. I already missed it. I was angry, of course, but I kinda wished I had grabbed a book of matches or something. Something to remember the place by. Cause I'd probably never go back in there. Not even for a drink.

I slid behind the wheel of the Caddy, lowered the drop top and pushed in the lighter. The lighter popped out and I lit a cigarette, took a couple quick puffs and wondered if I could maybe get away with it if I decided to wait for Mitch to come out and run him over. That might damage the Caddy, though. And anyway, hell, Mitch wasn't that bad. He didn't deserve to get run over to death. At least not by me.

I don't know, he might have done something really bad to someone else some time in his life. I didn't really know him all that well. But up until he fired me I thought he was a pretty good guy. And I suppose he still was.

What was I saying? Well, so anyway, I was crying like a damn baby, with tears blinding me and snot running all down my face. I'll admit it. And before I knew it, a police cruiser was pulling me over to the side of the road. I didn't even realize I had left Mitch's lot. That's how upset I was.

Police in this town are used to seeing grown men cry. But I suspect it would have been worse for me if I'd had out of state tags. Nobody has more reason to cry than the locals, and they know it. So I didn't seem so pathetic. The Officer didn't judge me any. I'd been weaving a bit on account of my blubbering, and I reckon he was just happy to see I wasn't drunk. He let me off with a warning, probably cause he had to. I let him pull around me before starting up and getting back on the road, myself. I had to let the cruiser get far enough ahead so I wouldn't follow it. Cause I would. It was something I'd done since I was a kid. If I saw a police car or an ambulance I'd follow it. I guess it made me feel like I was in the middle of something. Part of the world outside my own life, I guess. It's probably hard to understand, but it's even harder to explain, so I won't. I'd gotten into more trouble because of that than anything else, if you can believe it. I'll tell you something funny, though. If you ever want to be mistaken for a lawyer, all you have to do is drive too close to an ambulance.

That's all it takes to impersonate a lawyer. Never mind a fancy suit and college degree. I can tell you this, too… it takes a helluva lot more, and it's a helluva lot harder, to impersonate Elvis Pressley. Yes, sir.

# CHAPTER 2

I LIVE JUST about fifteen miles out of town. Not fifteen miles from city limits, understand. Fifteen miles from the center, I mean, which puts it square in hard luck territory. The neighborhood was new thirty years ago, but the houses weren't made all that well, and they're slowly but surely falling apart. I moved out to this area about eight years ago when apartments in the city got too expensive. I bought a small lot and put a trailer on it. Folks living in the houses got to look down their noses at me for a couple years before the desert finally wasted away their good homes. Sand and sun peeled the paint off of 'em and corroded the metal. Flash floods washed away their paving and rotted the wood. Did the same to my trailer, but trailers don't look all that great anyhow. Everybody seems to get along just fine now. I couldn't have better next door neighbors if I bought 'em from the store. It's the people we live with *inside* our homes that drive us crazy, not the people living next to 'em. Well, for me, anyway.

The worst thing about where I live is the awkward distance from town. It's mostly flatland so you can see downtown from the road, but it's still too far to walk in 115 degree heat. The highway runs perpendicular to my neighborhood and that's several miles away. What I'm getting to is this- at least once a week on my way home I'll spot some runaway kid. I'd say more than half of them are young girls. Most of 'em's probably eighteen, nineteen. But I've seen some you'd swear were just eleven or twelve. Most of 'em still hold up their signs-- 'LAS VEGAS'-- chicken scratched with a magic marker, as if as an afterthought. I don't put no judgment on them; poor kids probably never know where they're going when they run out on whatever was driving away at 'em. But still, they could put a little effort into it. Of course, the ones who do write a nice, neat little sign are the ones you have to question. If the sign is clean, they knew they were heading here from the beginning, they probably already got it in their heads to be a showgirl or stripper. They're already willing to sell it. Which makes it that much more depressing. Every time I drive by one, I start to feeling bad. There's just something about me that puts all those young girls in a bottle labeled 'innocence'. I'll take a few quick glances at 'em in the rearview mirror and think maybe I should stop for them. Give them a ride into town and try to dump every last bit of knowledge I can on 'em so's they can maybe live a nicer, cleaner, better life. But even then, I know I'm only a real bad day from being one of those people that does all the bad things to them you hope to never see done.

It's probably that I'm too sensitive. It hurts my heart a little to see anybody suffer. Makes it hard just to drive down the street sometimes. There's always somebody around who looks miserable. It gets to where all you can do is close your eyes to them; try and deny it however you can. But it's hard. And then there are the days you don't mind seeing the miserable people; when it doesn't take much of an effort to ignore them; well then... then you just feel worse later, knowing how easy it is for you to ignore the suffering of others. The only thing you can do then is roll down your window the next day and give up some change. Then you start wondering, what can be done? We need more shelters. More charities; and why can't this country find these people jobs? It gets to where you feel they're using their misery as a weapon against you. God-damned miserable people confront you with so much of the world's shit, it sometimes makes you want to slit their throats.

Sometimes it's hard to keep things in perspective. Luckily, though, I've always been pretty good at that. I hadn't had a very good day. Mitch had fired me and I was feeling sorry for myself. All of a sudden, having a bad day started to feel like having a bad last couple months. I was almost home. I just had to get home.

When I pulled into my drive, I had to hit the brakes in order not to slam into the red Buick parked in my driveway. My sunglasses flew off my face and smacked against the windshield.

"Damn," I wheezed.

I hopped out of the Caddy, slammed the door shut and looked down at the sandy haired little boy sitting on my front steps. The ten year old son of my ex-wife's sister. He was playing with some kind of hand held video game and didn't look up at me for a few seconds. A peppy, beepidy-bop tune sounded from the game.

"What the hell you doing here?" I asked.

The kid shrugged, turned his attention back to the game. *His eyes are too far apart. Creepy little bastard.*

"Where are your folks? They inside?"

He nodded.

"Inside? They went inside? Inside my home. Without asking, or even telling me ya'll were coming?" He didn't answer. I sighed. "What's that damn thing you're playing with?"

"It's called 'Bazooka Jones'," he said. "It's new, but I don't like it."

"Yeah? What's wrong with it?"

He gave another shrug. "I dunno. It's kind of stupid. It's new but it looks old. It looks like a game you would have played when you were a kid."

"Hand it here. Let me see." I reached out, snapping my fingers.

He handed me the game and said, quietly, "I'm not a dog."

"Prove it," I replied.

It did look like a game I would have played when I was a kid. Everything on the tiny screen was blocky, all squares and colorful. Almost an exact representation of how I viewed my past. I got a nice whiff of nostalgia. When I was a little boy I asked my grandmother for a Nintendo game consul for Christmas. She got one for my brother but not one for me. I remember screaming and hollering about it. I remember my grandma saying my brother would share it with me, but that didn't stop me screaming. My brother hadn't asked for it, and I had, yet he was the one who got it. I never could see that as anything but unjust. All the same, it's an embarrassing memory. I never could look my grandma in the eye after that.

"Pretty nice," I said, handing back the game. "Come on. Let's go find out what you're doing here." I opened the front door and motioned for him to follow.

"I'd rather wait out here," he said.

I went through the screen door and let it swing back hard. Maggie was sitting at the kitchen table, supposedly waiting for me. I imagined myself diving over the table and wrapping my hands around her neck. *Gonna squeeze until your head pops off! You're gonna be headless in Hell!*

"Evening, Maggie," I said, peering into the living room.

"Roger isn't here. He didn't come with us," Maggie said. Her eyes were glued to the floor. She looked, I don't know... sort of ashamed.

I sat down opposite her and waited for her to explain herself. I rubbed the calluses on the fingers of my right hand and tried not to look at her. If I looked at her at all, I'd just be staring at her tits. I knew that much about myself. "You two splitting up again?" I asked, making a fist and observing the veins pushing out the back of my hand.

"It's for good this time."

"Um-hum."

"I mean it, god damn it. I ain't never going back to

that son of a bitch. I swear to god."

I leaned back in my chair, balancing on the back two legs with my knees braced under the table. "Well, that's fine, Maggie. But, um… what's that kid's name again?" I jerked my thumb toward the door.

"Sam."

"Well, Maggie, don't you think you and Sam would be better off hiding out at your sister's house? I mean… it's a little peculiar you coming by here without any warning. You and I aren't family any more. Haven't been family in years." I said this as evenly as I could. I've always had a nice, even tempered way of speaking to people. I find it lowers their defenses and, hopefully, helps them to enjoy being around me.

Her mouth dropped open and she tried to look shocked, or hurt. "F-Frank…"

"How'd you get in, anyway? Where did you get a key?"

"M-Mary-Anne gave me a key before you divorced and I just n-never threw it out."

"Well how about that. No, really. That's just swell. Why, I--"

Maggie jumped out of her chair and came at me with quick, shuffling bird steps. She grabbed hold of me and buried her face in my jacket and started crying like I've never heard a woman cry before. And I mean that. I stretched my head back as far as I could to keep my face away from her. My eyes fell on the pale line in her scalp where the parts in her hair separate. Flakes of dried skin mixed in with her bright red hair, down near the light brown roots. I could imagine what her tears were doing to my jacket, all that saline. I held my hands out, sort of letting 'em hover over her shoulders. Any touching on my part would be a commitment. Either I was going to be her shoulder to cry on, or I was going to tell her to hit the road. A part of me wanted to reach down and rip her blouse open. See what color bra she had on.

*They're right there in front of you!*

"Now. Now. Maggie. It'll be alright. Everything will be okay," I said, patting her on the back. "Calm down, now. There ain't no use in crying. Now you just sit back down and tell me what's happened. I'll try and help out the best I can."

*I'll bet she's got sweet little pink nipples. Oh, God.*

"Just sit yourself back down and... pull yourself together. Christ's sake, Maggie. What happens if your boy sees you like this? How am I supposed to explain anything to him?"

"I don't know what to do anymore," she kept on. She shrugged and waved her hands in front of me, her eyes wild. "It's really over this time. I don't think I could go back even if I wanted to."

"Come on now, Maggie. I'm sure it's not that bad. Heck. You and Roger have had some pretty hefty spats and you always managed to patch things up before."

She shook her head erratically. "Not this time," she said; then once more. "Not this time."

I didn't think there was anything funny about the way she was acting, but I went ahead and laughed anyway. "What's so different this time?"

"Wh--uh…well, I-- I-I…we g-got into one of our a-arguments," she began crying again, and her nose swelled up pretty big, making her words come out funny. "And he s-started smacking me around again… and I-- I grabbed a kitchen knife, and-- and then I kind of went blank"

"You went blank…?"

"Um-huh. Yeah."

"…And what?"

"And c-chopped off four of his fingers."

Now what was I supposed to say to that?

"I just don't t-think that the marriage can recover from that."

"Nope. Yeah, you're probably right. You're marriage probably should not recover from something like that," I said. And she went on crying, but at least she'd gotten quiet about it. "Damn, Maggie. Whew. Does the boy know you cut half his dad's damn hand off?"

"Don't be s-silly. Of course not."

Now, I should tell you, I'd always been, well, I'll just go ahead and say it… extremely sexually attracted to Maggie. The whole time I was married to Mary-Anne I thought about Maggie, sexually. It seemed like every day I'd come up with some kind of crazy scenario that would lead to the two of us having sex. But I never had the gumption to realize any of those fantasies. That, and I ain't no two-timing son-of-a-bitch.

However, after what she'd just told me, the sexual attraction lessened a bit. I didn't like the idea of her taking a knife to her husband's digits. I didn't like the picture it put in my mind. Cut off fingers were a little too close to a cut off dong. And I'd already had enough issues in that department. The first time I ever came close to having real, full blown sex with a girl, back when I was seventeen years old, I couldn't get a hard on. Yeah, I don't know. It gives me cold sweats just remembering it. The girl, her name was Lori, was a real looker too. I remember just how she looked. About five foot seven, with medium short blonde hair, cut just above the shoulders. Blue eyes. I'd say she weighed maybe one hundred and ten pounds. She had the second biggest pair of titties I'd ever seen in real life. The biggest I'd ever seen belonged to a girl named Carmen; Carmen something or other, and she was in my seventh grade home room class. I swear, it was like one day she didn't have them and the next day she did and they were the biggest damn things I'd ever seen in my life… at that time. The boy's would pay her five, ten bucks to lift up her shirt behind the gymnasium and give 'em a peek. I never did, though. I never had the gumption for that sort of thing. And, now that I think about it, Carmen's breasts probably weren't all that big. It's just that she was the first girl I'd ever seen blossom, and naturally, them being the first titties other than my mother's I'd ever sat next to, they retain a much larger space in my memory. So yeah, I guess Lori really had the biggest titties I'd ever seen. And I guess that intimidated me a bit. Her looking so pretty and having such big, big titties. We'd snuck way out in the woods away from everybody. We made out for a while before taking off our clothes. I remember wondering why the hell my privates weren't responding to the stimulus. I couldn't understand it. Lori was right there, naked in all her glory just staring down at me, but nothing was happening. I remember her saying "Well?" and me tugging on it a bit to get it working. But the more I messed with it, the less I could feel. Almost like I was just playing with my loose elbow skin. I remember asking her to "Suck on it a little, would you?" but she just shook her head no. Shook her head and smiled kind of. Like she thought it was funny. Like she was thinking right then and there how she was going to be relieved the next day by not having fucked me. Well, I'll tell you. If I could have gotten it up right then, I probably would have raped her. And she'd have deserved it, I think. Smiling the way she did. I just couldn't believe my night was turning out that way. What the fuck had I done to deserve that? It wasn't even my idea to have sex. It was all hers. It was her idea to trek way out in the damn woods. And now I had to follow along behind her all the way back, with my head held low, not even able to look at the back of her head. I walked to a friend's house after seeing her home and knocked on his door. He'd known what my plans were that night, and when he opened the door, I could see the expectation on his face. He'd been excited for me. But I just shook my head and said "I couldn't do it." Even back then I was just too honest of a person to keep that kind of shit to myself.

Damn. Lori. I hadn't thought of her in years. And Carmen. Whatever happened to the two of them, I wonder. Lori's probably doing alright. She was too shrewd not to. But Carmen. Well, I'd be surprised if she hadn't killed herself a long time ago. It must really mess you up being the first girl your age to grow breasts. I'd never really thought about that till just now.

"W-what am I going to do?" Maggie pleaded.

"Well, Maggie," I said, shaking my head to loosen my thoughts, interlocking my fingers behind my neck, "have you ever heard it said, that if you ever see a white dog, you should keep your mouth shut until you see a white horse?"

She shook her head.

"Back when I was a boy, my daddy used to say that all the time. And, well, I guess originally I thought it was just his way of telling me to hush up, me or my mother, or whoever was getting on his nerves. But now, Maggie, it seems to me to be saying 'Hold still. Show a little patience. Don't be rash.' You understand what I'm saying?"

Her head moved in what could be called a circular motion, as if unsure whether to nod for 'yes' or shake for 'no', until finally she blurted out, "I'm not sure."

And the way she said it, it was like I was the one making her life difficult. I looked away from her, lit a cigarette and sighed.

# CHAPTER 3

I ALMOST rolled off the couch when I woke up. Twisted my wrist a bit catching myself, and hugged the cushion with my knees, but it was alright. It took probably a full minute to figure out what I was doing there. I'd had to give up my bed to Maggie. It was the least I could do, really. I'm just that kind of guy, I suppose. I imagine most men are the same way, but then again, maybe not. One thing's for sure, women aren't.

I flipped my legs off the couch and sat for a while, watching the dust motes swim in the early light seeping through the window shade, then stood up and walked to the bathroom. I never have much on my mind when I wake up. I'd never been what you might call a morning person, but I'd never been much of anything right after waking, no matter what time of day or night. Just always been that way. I seem to respond to things instinctively, without foresight or anything like that. If I woke up and the house was on fire, I'd get out of the house, but not because I needed to get away from the fire so much as that it just wouldn't be where I wanted to be. But uh...

As I do every morning, I filled the sink halfway up with cold water, then put my face in the water for a few seconds. After lifting back up, I stare at myself in the mirror and then give a good scream. It's not so much something I do on purpose. It's just something I do. After that I'm bright as fireworks. As awake as can be.

When I made my way to the living room, Maggie was sitting on the couch. I don't know if I woke her up or if she got up on her own accord, but there she was. I slumped down next to her and rubbed my eyes. She yawned.

"It didn't occur to me last night," I said. "But there's a good chance the police are after you."

"I'd thought about that," she said, her voice kind of deadpan. It was hard to tell if she was naturally dispassionate, or not yet fully awake. But ain't it always like that with women? I grunted.

"Then again, they haven't come knocking yet."

"Marie-Anne would have told me something."

"How's that?"

"She woulda called."

"Not here she wouldn't."

"Sure. Why wouldn't she?"

I turned real slow to look at her. *You fucking cunt! If that bitch calls here and I have to hear the sound of her voice you will fucking regret it!*

I harrumphed good naturedly. "Well, how's she supposed to know you'd come here?"

"Oh, right," Maggie said. She chuckled a bit, kind of embarrassed. "I guess that's why I came here. Cause nobody would think of it."

"Yeah, but still…" I stood up and stretched, then jumped a little when I heard the bathroom door shut.

"I didn't think he'd wake up this early," Maggie said. "Is it all right for him to take a bath?"

"Course it's all right," I answered. "I'm gonna grab a few things out of the bedroom real quick."

She knocked on the bathroom door to let Sam know he could take a bath and I went back to my bedroom. Sam had either made the bed or slept so soundly he hadn't moved. The blankets I'd let Maggie use were bundled in the corner next to the bed. I smiled. She'd let the boy take the bed and slept on the floor herself. They could have both fit in the bed, but I guess she'd wanted him to be as comfortable as he could be away from his own home. I was glad to see that. It was sweet.

I grabbed a change of clothes from the dresser, tossed them on the bed and took off the clothes I'd slept in. Then I picked up the pillow Maggie had used, slipped the pillow case off, held it up to my face and inhaled deeply. I masturbated into the pillow case real quick, like thirty seconds quick, then bundled it with my dirty clothes before changing into the clean ones. I put the bundle of dirty clothes under my arm and went back out to the living room.

"I don't have much in the way of breakfast, but there's cereal and, I think…" I tossed the dirty clothes on the kitchen floor and looked in the refrigerator, "milk. Or, there's a Denny's right down the street." I took the cap off the milk and sniffed. It was still good. "It's up to you." I closed the refrigerator door and sort of hovered, shuffled around in front of it, saying, "Um," and "Huh," searching for a pretext to leave the house. I didn't think I owed her a lie by saying I had to be at work, but I didn't really want her knowing the truth either. I had to find another job. I scooped the dirty clothes up from the floor. "You and Sam will be okay on your own for a little while right?"

Maggie hesitated, turned down her bottom lip and lifted her hands. Obviously she hadn't thought of the possibility of maybe being left alone. "I guess so," she said, finally.

"Okay. Good." I grabbed my car keys, turned first to the left, then to the right, almost as if I'd forgotten where the front door was and, well, I guess I had. "Yeah," I said. "Okay. Be back after work." It was automatic, and as soon as I said it I wanted to slap myself on the head.

I threw the dirty clothes on the floorboard of the passenger side and sat for a while before turning the key in the ignition. As soon as I stepped outside, the reality of unemployment hit me and all my soon to be troubles glared down at me, riding on the heat of the sun and burning me to a crisp on my white leather seats. You can believe it or not, but I hadn't been unemployed for almost a decade. It began to dawn on me just how lucky I was when I got that job with Mitch. Now I didn't know what to do. It was scary.

I started the car. The radio came on and straightaway cheered me up. Terry Stafford's version of 'Suspicion' played. Right from the beginning, almost as if it had been queued up and waiting for me. Now, I'll go ahead and admit it, but I've always liked Terry Stafford's version better. In fact, I believe most people do, they either just won't admit it, or they think ol' Terry *is* Elvis, in which case, they aren't so hard on themselves. Nobody seems to have that problem with 'Blue Suede Shoes', but I imagine it's because Carl Perkins cut his version first. Now that I think about it, I guess it really is all about originality. You can love Elvis Pressley as much as you want, but if you think his version of 'Reddy Teddy' is better than Little Richard's, there's something wrong with you. Yes, sir. There's just something about Stafford's version, makes me feel good inside.

The song was over before I joined with the main road into town, but I was enjoying it so much I turned off the radio and played it again in my head over and over until I did get into town. By the time I found a parking spot and collected my ticket I'd almost forgotten why I was there at all. I walked down the street, taking it easy on myself at first, looking at adverts placed in the windows, before walking into clubs at random and asking if they needed anybody to fill a spot. By this time, the only part of the song playing in my head was the bass line and the bop, but that was still pretty good.

And, well, I don't see any reason to give you the details of why I didn't find a job that day. I imagine there wouldn't be no story for you to read if I had found one. I did do a lot of searching, and I tried real hard. By the end of the day I'd probably spent more time out of doors in that city since moving there. I almost got heat stroke. I avoided it by going into one of the casinos. I practically ran to the bathroom. I splashed water on my face and head, put my mouth under the faucet and took a few gulps, then threw up in the sink. It's pretty bad when your body rejects water.

I rinsed my mouth out, combed my hair back, and tried to make myself look somewhat presentable before leaving the bathroom. I tried to avoid the employees as I made for the casino doors, but I made the mistake of making eye contact with one of the waitresses. "Damn it all," I muttered, realizing I was going to have to stick around now. It's something I've always disliked about myself, but I've never been able to walk into a place of business and leave without buying something, anything. I've bought I don't know how much useless bullshit in my life for that very reason. If I go to the corner store for cigarettes and they don't have my brand, I buy a soda and a beef jerky just so the guy behind the counter won't think I'm boycotting the place. I also have a problem buying things in singles. I have to at least buy two or three things. If I go to buy toilet paper, even if that's all I need, I'll spend a half hour, at least, looking for something else to buy along with it. It's just another one of my quirks, I guess.

I searched out the nickel slots and sat down, ordered a beer from the waitress that had spotted me, and burped a couple times, tasting the acid reflux. After making change with the waitress when she brought my beer, I had about six nickels to play with. I figured that'd last me about five minutes, unless I won jackpot. I checked my watch with each pull of the lever.

Roughly five minutes later I was out cursing on the sidewalk.

Now, I'm gonna get cynical.

It was a mistake sitting down in front of a slot machine. As soon as a man decides to gamble he reveals himself as a wishful thinker. I may not have been exactly truthful by saying I was at the slots just to waste time. Honestly, I could have wasted five minutes at the bar, or even just walking around. I could have chatted with the waitress, or counted stains on the carpet, but I didn't. No, sir, I had to play something. Heh, I'm not even sure how much a nickel slot pays out, but, yeah, I was hoping to win. Of course I was.

So anyway, I kicked the curb and rubbed the back of my neck and was feeling sorry for myself. I looked up and down the strip and wanted to kick the shit out of every fat Elvis I saw. Of course, you don't see as many now as you once did, but they're still around; most of them, it seems, stand outside the small souvenir shops, waving people inside, like glorified hobo's; but at least they got a damn job.

In all my years playing this town, I met only one other '*early*' Elvis. Raymond Waters. I looked to see if his information was still in my phone. Finding it, I gave him a call. You see, being an *Early* Elvis is like being a left hander, it's a small club, and it sticks together. He agreed to meet me at a buffet diner- a fifties themed diner, of course- not far from where I already was. In fact, he was already there, so it really wasn't any problem for him.

"Jesus, God," I said, taking a seat opposite Raymond in the shiny red booth.

He looked up from his plate, knife in one hand, fork in the other, smiled and huffed a laugh at me. I leaned my head against the window and tapped my fingers over the tiny decoration jukebox on the table.

"What's up, Frank. What's eating you?"

I shook my head and rubbed my eyelids. "What is this?" I asked.

"What's what?"

"This. This," I said, sliding his- not one, but five plates around close to the edge of the table. "What is this?"

I flicked some mashed potatoes at him.

"Hey! Hey," he said, dropping his fork and pointing a finger at me threateningly. "Cut it out." He sighed, then grinned, showing his teeth. "So what's eating you? Really, what's the matter? You sounded pretty bad on the phone."

I stared at his lip. Raymond had that curl to his upper lip, just like Elvis, and it was natural too. That used to burn me up.

"It's funny you should ask, Ray. It looks like you've caught a bit of the bug that's put me under the weather. Well, maybe not yet. You don't look nearly as bad as me, but I can see you've been warned of the symptoms."

He held out his hands and lifted his brow.

I paused a moment. Just stared at the plates of food in front of us.

"Trying to pack on some pounds, eh, Ray?"

"Pack on pounds, hell," he said with a sneer. "Take a look at me, Frank." He wrapped his left hand around his right wrist. The thumb and pinky came together. "I ain't nothing but metabolism. I eat this much to survive, never mind gaining weight."

"Bullshit."

"Fuck you, bullshit."

"I used to look up to you, man."

"Oh, you can still look up to me," he replied, spooning some mac and cheese to his mouth. "I've still got my gig. I'll put you on the list. Put you right up by center stage."

I moaned. "Man, that's cold blooded."

"Yeah. You're right. Shit. Well, hey… I apologize."

*Damn it. His accent is perfect!*

I never was all that great with my aural impersonation… not with regular speech. Singing was one thing, but speaking was a whole different ball-game. I never could perfect that Deep South honky slur like the King had. Hell, nobody else really had it. Not even the other members of the Memphis Mafia. But Raymond, he had it. Had it down pat.

"Really, Frank, I didn't mean anything by it. In all serious, man, I have been a little nervous, myself, after hearing you got canned. That's why I'm here stuffing my face. So Riley won't ambush me the way Mitch did you." He snorted. "You should see what I got in the trunk of my car, man. God damn wigs and sequined suits. I got a cane with a big shiny silver thing on top. Cost me a damn fortune. Man, it's ridiculous." He paused. "I do kind of like the cane, though."

"What's the world coming to, Ray?"

"Heck if I know."

"Doesn't seem fair, you know?--um… couple of jerks like us, though. Heh… who are we to expect people to give us money for doing what we love to do, right? Maybe we should put on the jump suits and stupid gold rings. I don't know… maybe those guys that do that deserve the money, because they're doing shit they wouldn't normally do. That's like a real job, right? What a job is supposed to be. Wearing some silly costume... prancing around like an idiot. Playing the f-fool..."

"Hey, Frank. Jesus," Raymond cut in, pushing himself back against his seat. "You okay, man?"

"Huh? What? I don't know. I don't know what I'm talking about. Don't listen to me."

"Frank. Frank, you just blew chunks up all over the table."

"Huh?" I wiped my chin and looked down. He was right. There was a spray pattern of brownish vomit covering all five of Raymond's lunch plates, seeping into his mashed potatoes and discoloring the broccoli. It collected in a small, meatier pool between my hands on the table. Watery brown beads clung to the hairs on my forearms.

"Uhh...Oh, my god," I groaned, swiveling my head. I covered my mouth with one hand and waved the other in front of me. "Man, I am so sorry. That's disgusting. I don't know what came over me. Jesus H. Christ."

Air whistled through Raymond's bottom teeth as he gave a sympathetic grimace. He covered his nose. "Man, that's foul."

"I-I-I'll just get t-this cleaned up, Ray. Uh... no big deal..."

"No big deal?" Raymond started fiddling with his shirt. He popped off one of the lower buttons. "Frank, you look like hell. You should see a doctor."

"N-no. It's nothing, Ray. J-just nerves, is all."

"Whatever it is--"

"My goodness. What happened here?" exclaimed the waitress, coming by on one of her rounds. She looked thoroughly disgusted.

"It n-nothing..." I said, beginning to make an excuse. Her presence immediately frustrated me, making me angry. I found her mildly attractive and that made my accident all the more embarrassing. A pretty girl was smelling my stink.

"I'll tell you what's happened, god-damn it!" Ray shouted. "A button! There was a button in my food and I damn near choked on it."

Unbeknownst to me, Raymond had planted the button into the pool of vomit. That same button, he was now holding out in front of the waitress after lifting it from my sick. "Can you believe this, Frank? I eat here once a week and they try to kill me with a button."

The waitress fidgeted nervously. She pulled a white towel from her apron and dangled it over the pool of vomit, holding it between her thumb and index finger, and dropped it over the most concentrated area. "Sir. Sir, I don't know what to say. I'm sure there is some explanation. I-I, hurnh--!" she gagged a bit and moved away. Tears welled in her eyes, making her even prettier in mine. Glassy eyes always did something for me. I looked down at the name on her tag. "Stifanie".

"Forget it, miss," Raymond snapped. "Just bring the check and let me get the hell out of here."

"T-that's okay," said Stifanie. "D-don't worry about the c-check, sir. Don't be ridiculous. Of course we're more than sorry."

Raymond seemed to relax, then. He let a sly smile play on his lips. "On the house, huh? Well, hell, I guess that's alright." He got up and slid by her. "Well, I guess there's no real harm done. I reckon we can just all of us go on about the rest of our day, and move on with our lives. How about you?"

Stifanie sniffed and forced a smile. I inhaled deeply while scooting by her and tried to keep my mouth closed so she wouldn't smell the vomit on my breath. I stood by the door and marveled as Raymond slipped the girl his business card. He was all smiles now. He didn't seem to care that he was supposed to have just thrown up all over the place to extricate a button. He was leaving the situation with a free meal and... and, fucking possibly a date with Stifanie, the waitress. The man was a stud.

"Sure you're feeling alright?" he asked me, slipping his jacket on and following me to the parking lot. "I've got some antacids in my glove compartment."

"That's okay. I've got some of my own." We all did; at least everyone I've ever known who has been on stage. I grabbed a chewable capsule from my pocket and tossed it in my mouth. Indigestion wasn't the problem, I knew that, but a Rolaids would help with the stink breath.

"So what's it gonna be?" he asked, leaning against his car. "What'd you want to see me for?"

I stared off down the strip, ashamed to meet his eye for some reason. Well, I guess I was embarrassed. "Aw, forget about it. It's nothing."

"Come on, Chief. By the look on your face, it ain't

nothing that's bothering you."

*Well, Ray, put it to you like this. It ain't bad enough I've lost my job; but my ex sister-in-law, you remember Mary-Anne's sister, Margaret? Yeah, so she shows up with her son... little smart assed fucking prick he is, let me tell you... just like his dad. So I don't know if I should just tell them to get lost, or what. Cause I can't afford no bottom feeders, right? I mean, who can in this economy? So I don't necessarily think I'd be doing the wrong thing if I gave them the boot, but, well, it seems Maggie's done something pretty stupid, and it might mean, well, she might be in some kind of trouble with the law... and, if not the law, she's still probably in for a pretty good ass kicking in the near future... either way... it seems she's not on the road to good times, however you want to look at it... and, well, shit... I guess I'm just a little concerned is all. I mean, hell, I've always rooted for the underdog, I'd say, and I guess, I feel like if I could help her out in some way, I might as well do just that. What do you think? But then, I am a little anxious this might stir up some bad things with regards to that... whore, Mary-Anne.*

"It's nothing, Ray," I said. "I'm just bummed out over losing the gig. Guess I was just looking for a— uh, a pep talk, or some shit."

"Yeah, I'd like to help, Frank, but the truth is you won't find another sweet gig like Mitch's for a while. Not around here, you won't."

"Um-hum."

"Makes you appreciate the little things."

"Yep."

"But I guess in this town, anything that comes with a steady paycheck is a sweet ride."

"I suppose you're right."

"It could be like this, Frank; the King's had his day. Hell, he's been gone over thirty years. All the people who grew up on him are older than shit right now. Ain't no one around to be touched by the nostalgia no more."

"What are you trying to say, Ray?"

He shrugged. "Just saying... maybe we should move on to Springsteen."

"Hunh," I smiled. "That'll be over my dead body, man."

"We can put on make-up and start a Kiss cover band. What do you say, Frank?"

"I say I'll catch you later, Jack." I walked to the Caddy.

"Sure. Just go with the flow, Joe," he called after me.

I drove around for a couple hours after that. Finished off the pint of gin I kept in the glove box. I kept checking the time, even though I didn't have anywhere to be. It was one of those times when five minutes feel like five hours. You know what I'm talkin' about, you've been there.

That's essentially how it happened. There wasn't any plan, or even any real thought behind it. I still don't know what made me do it. In retrospect, it probably wasn't one of my better decisions. But the way I figured it, the man had a right to know where his wife and kid were, right. So, anyway, I pulled off the road at the convenience store just up the street to my house, stumbled over to the pay phone and lifted the receiver. I dialed Maggie's husband and, well, before I really knew what I was doing I was telling him 'not to god damn worry who it is mother fucker and if you ever want to see your boy alive again and in one fucking piece you'll hang tight and wait for my next call.'

And that was that.

# CHAPTER 4

I WASN'T FOR sure if Raymond had been joking or not, but if he really thought there was money to be had from a Kiss cover band, he was crazy. I once knew a guy whose cousin was in a Beatles cover band and, on alternating weekends when he wasn't playing a gig, he was managing a two-bit burger joint one block from his apartment. The thought of it sent chills up my spine. I figure if a man can't make a living covering Lennon and McCartney, he ain't got a chance in hell with Kiss. It kind of pissed me off that Raymond had even suggested it. Even if it had been a joke, it wasn't funny.

I pulled against the curb in front of my house, put the car in park, and shuffled through the CD's in my glove box. I only had one Springsteen album, a Greatest Hits I picked up a long time ago when I was feeling nostalgic for the 80's for some reason. Shit. Well, yeah. I put the CD in the player, skimmed through a couple songs and tried to get a feel for them; tried to imagine myself up on a stage performing them; tried to imagine earning a paycheck off of it. It was hard to say. But I did notice I was bobbing my head to some of the tunes. That's about the time I slapped myself in the face.

*What the fuck are you thinking?*

What the fuck was I thinking? *Come on, Frank. Snap out of it. Yeah, you're a bit scared. A little bit shaky. A little bit panicked. But you're just going to have to face facts. The King is the King, and playing anybody else is a cover band. You're no cover artist, dude, you're an ar-teest. You do Elvis Pressley, man, and there ain't nothing else to say about that. And if you can't do Elvis, you're just going to have to starve to death because you don't want to live in a world that don't want to see the King reincarnated on a nightly basis, for no cover charge and just a two drink minimum, and all the atmosphere that goes along with it. A man like Elvis has got to live forever, Frank. And you're the special kind of person to make it happen.*

Yeah, I guess.

I killed the engine and hopped out of the Caddy. I stared long and hard at Maggie's red Buick before going into the house. She was sitting on the couch watching television. All the windows were closed and the blinds pulled down so the only light in the room came from the box. I stood in the front hallway, letting my eyes adjust, and tossed my keys to where I guessed they would hit the kitchen counter. Maggie looked over with a glazed look in her eye. She smiled but her eyes didn't get any clearer. I sniffed.

"Is that pot?" I asked, knowing for a damn fact that it was.

"Um-hum. You don't have a problem with it do you?" she said, barely nodding.

I pulled a cigarette from my half empty pack and lit it. I blew a great cloud of smoke into the living room and watched it flatten and hover, glowing blue from the light of the television, at just about the height of my neck. "Well, yes I do, Mags. It stinks. It permeates, you know?" I said.

"I'm sorry," she said, quietly, almost mumbling. "I never think about that anymore."

"Yeah, I know," I replied. "You ask me, that's why most of you pot-heads get hassled by the law the way you do. That shit being so common and easy to procure, the average reefer addict just plain forgets he's breaking the law."

Maggie made a choking sound; one of those strained ironic laughs, and looked up at me. "Are you being serious?"

I exhaled another layer of smoke into the room, paused for a moment, then smiled. "Heck, Mags. I guess not. But turn a fan on or something. It really does stink."

Her snicker gave way to a giggle. "My smoke smells better than your smoke."

The image flashed into my mind, of me grabbing her by the face and scooping her eyeball out with my thumb. But I couldn't do a thing like that. Instead I just laughed it off. I didn't want to offend her or hurt her feelings. "I guess it just depends on what you're used to," I said.

"That's why they invented air fresheners," said Maggie.

"Yeah," I said. "Yeah. You're right. We're..." and I couldn't help but notice my words spacing themselves out, "You. Just. Don't. Care."

Maggie rolled her head along the back of the couch until her face was directly in front of mine. I looked into her glassy green eyes and felt her breath on my face. There was maybe an inch, an inch and a half distance between us and I fought the urge to pull my head back or close my eyes. The light from the television created a perfect outline in shadow of her breasts through her white t-shirt and-

She made that choked, ironic sound again that is the pot-head's laughter. A little bit of spittle hit my face and she doubled over on the couch, holding her stomach.

I stared at her, wiped my cheek. "Maggie. Where is Sam?"

She gasped and sputtered, still clutching her stomach. Tears streamed down her cheeks, her face flushed red. I snapped my fingers in front of her face. "Hey. Where's your kid?"

Her eyes focused on my snapping fingers, and she forced herself to sit up. She took several deep breaths. "Wh- what the hell did you do that for?"

"Seriously now, Maggie. It's getting a little old."

"H- huh?"

"I can tolerate a little pot, Mags, but I can't handle the crazy laughter. I feel like you're kind of laughing at me and it makes me uncomfortable."

She massaged her abdomen and stared blankly down at the floor. "I'm sorry," she said, kind of childlike. Like I'd caught her stealing cookies from the cookie jar. Her bottom lip even pushed out a little, quivered a little.

I realized I was sneering but I didn't quite know why. I gripped the lower half of my face in my hand and tried my best to mold myself a smile. "Well, now, doggone, Maggie. I already told you it's not a big deal. Just remember, though, everything in moderation." I slapped her on the thigh. "I can deal with a little marijuana stink and a little bit of silliness, just don't make me feel like a shit ass when there's nothing I can laugh along with." She continued to stare blankly, but gave what I interpreted as a nod in the positive. "Now where's that little scallywag of yours gotten off to?"

Now, I won't lie and say I was worried he'd get himself into trouble, or get hurt playing in the street, or the open fields out back, maybe scrape his knee on some old rusted metal and have to get taken to the emergency room for a shot. Although I would've hated to see anything like that happen. No, I think even then I was kinda sorta putting a plan together way in the back of my head. Something, probably along the lines of what you may or may not have already read about. I don't know. It's kind of creepy isn't it?

Maggie jerked her thumb in the air, indicating the back room. My room. "He's been cooped up back there for hours."

"Sleeping?"

"I don't know. Probably. He's been real quiet."

"Hmm."

"What?"

"Ah… it's nothing. I was just thinking."

"About what?"

"About… maybe we should do something about your car. I've got a--"

"Like what?" she asked, interrupting me.

Involuntarily, I showed my teeth. "I've got a tarp in

the work shed out back. I was thinking we should cover the car, just in case somebody comes looking for you. You know, on the off chance Dillon did call the authorities."

"The authorities?" Maggie sat up, her eyes finally coming to focus. "I never figured he'd call the police."

I stared. "You didn't?"

"Well, no. Not really. Well, I guess I didn't think about it all that much. But I guess I just thought he'd come looking for me, himself. Or, at least come after Sam."

Oddly, my knees began to buckle. There was something about the conversation that was putting me off ease. I felt like an underachiever at a family reunion. Like I was trying to hold a smile too long and my tendons were about to snap. I'd never been very good at manipulation. I didn't like it. "Well, Mags. He may not have had too much choice in the matter. He almost certainly went to the emergency room for his hand. To get his fingers sewed back on, or something, whatever the hell they'd do. Something like that is bound to garner attention and, well, maybe the doctors had to report it to the police just out of procedure. Either way, I think it best we cover your car with the tarp. At least that way, we won't get no surprises."

Maggie was silent for a moment. I couldn't tell if she were thinking of something to say, or floating back into her high. Then, she said, "I guess this means I'll be sticking around here for a while?"

"For the time being. Sure," I said, bobbing my

head, my hands on my hips. "I can't very well leave you to chance now, can I?"

She smiled.

I instantly got an erection.

There was something real nice about her smile. It was the way one of her eyeteeth peeked out from under the top lip to press into the bottom lip.

Strangely enough, this sexual attraction was the one single reason I had doubts about keeping her around. It certainly was not *the* reason for keeping her around. You had better believe that. No, sir. I never chased after, nor ever did anything out of the ordinary for no pussy. Never in my life. Chasing after pussy is like chasing after a brick wall on a rocket. I just never understood it, how so many people could allow themselves to be run down to the bone for those... parts. It's just... heh... I'll just. Well, I'll just say, I don't think anybody...

*Gets it, god damn it, I'm trying to tell you something here.*

...ever starts out in life, knowing how much of a damn tragedy we're going to turn our lives into, all for the sake of something that don't hardly ever last longer than ten minutes at a time. I think that's why most people... not all, but most people, think of children and childhood as something sacred. Sacred and pure. Something to be cherished and held onto, for as long as possible. Because when it's gone, it's gone, no matter who takes it from you.

"I'm gonna go check on Sam," I said, sticking my hand in the air in a half-assed wave and, realizing how unnecessary it was, I bit my lip and head for the bedroom.

Sam had made a big ball out of the blankets I'd set aside for Maggie, at the foot of my bed, and was slumped right down in the middle of them. He was hunched at the stomach, his shoulders drooping in that pose I had more or less learned meant he was in the middle of one of his video games. The colorful images on the tiny screen reflected in his eye glasses, and his lips moved quickly and elaborately, as if he were cursing whatever it was on the screen he was up against.

"I don't see how you do it," I said, standing at the entrance to the room. "The damn thing is the size of a cell phone. How can you distinguish anything?"

"This thing has great resolution," he responded.

I inched up behind him to watch his progress. He kept right on playing. I took this to mean I wasn't disturbing him. I watched his fingers manipulate tiny buttons I couldn't even see as he maneuvered a pink gorilla (I assumed he was the gorilla) from the left to the right of the screen. Black, skull faced things ran at the gorilla, coming in from the right, and each time they approached, the gorilla lifted a giant (respectively) forearm to squash them with its fist. Each skull faced creature folded like an accordion before disappearing and being replaced with a blinking number. The game seemed to go on this way for quite a while, with an added obstacle every now and then, of a car the gorilla had to jump over, or a racing hurdle, until finally, the gorilla commandeered a submarine which seemed to mark the end of that level.

"Holy shit," I gasped in amazement.

"I told you," Sam said, continuing on to the next level. Level 5.

I straightened up. "How many levels in this game?"

"Um. I think 42."

"You going to go through all 42 right now?"

"Ah. I dunno. Maybe," he shrugged. He didn't really seem to give a damn either way. But he was certainly willing to play through the entire game, apparently, just for the hell of it. Something like that is chilling in its own way, don't you think? At least to me. But what do I know? I guess what it was, as I saw the kid's spine protruding through his shirt, was a little bit of jealousy on my part. I was about as skinny as Sam when I was his age. But the world didn't seem to like skinny kids back then. Now I'm not talking just thin. When I say skinny I mean skinny. Like concentration camp skinny. When I was a kid, if you were skinny, you were either a bookworm, which meant being habitually pushed around, called a wimp, nerd, pussy, being laughed at by the girls, or you tried your hardest to act like you weren't skinny, and tried to play the rough sports with the bigger kids, and wound up being pushed around, called a wimp or a pussy, and being laughed at by the girls. Most of the skinny kids my age were just putting on a show. They weren't tough or smart. And now who the hell knows where *they* are in life. Probably spending a fortune on therapy and being bullied by their healthier and better adjusted children. I looked at Sam's protruding spine and sighed. The boy had come along in this world at exactly the right time. He could play that video game for hours without worrying about asthma or allergies, and without being considered shuttered or abnormal for it. It seemed like nobody really played contact sports anymore, and if they did, who gave a damn? Most everybody spends all day in front of a computer, whether at school or at home, so everybody's eyes are being screwed up. Everybody needs glasses. Sam had probably never been called "four eyes" in all his life. And, hey, let's face it, it's probably not such a bad thing to be too skinny in a world increasingly dominated by the Chinky-Chinese.

I'll also admit I felt a little less put off by the boy after seeing how basic the game was he played. Size of the screen and resolution aside, the pink gorilla was a lot closer to the kind of games I played growing up than I expected any kid Sam's age to be playing. I guess I figured he'd be playing one of those games you always hear about on the news that gives some kid epileptic fits, causes them to fall over and crack their head on a shelf, flop around like a fish and choke on their own vomit. Or maybe one of those games where the whole point of it is to build an alternate life. Not really a game, I suppose. But I guess it does take some kind of strategy to play it well. A few months earlier, I had read on the internet about some Korean couple whose baby girl starved to death while they were busy playing an 'alternate life' game. They were so immersed in the game, they completely neglected their own infant daughter as it wasted away, feeding off its own body until there was nothing left. After reading about that, I found myself wondering some things; the first was your basic gut reaction- how horrible can it get, why is humanity so disgusting, what's wrong with us, etc., etc. And I wondered if the couple were playing the 'alternate life' game together, were they a couple in their alternate lives; were they perfect parents, or were they two wholly different personality types. Was the male playing a female, and the woman playing a male? Was one of them playing a schoolteacher, and the other a naughty student? Was one of them a North Korean and the other from the South, and did they spent their time in the game castigating one another, telling the other how horrible he/she was? Were they at least winning the fucking game?

I pulled out the top drawer of my dresser and lifted out the black, hard plastic case containing my .38 Smith & Wesson. I removed the revolver from the case and made sure Sam hadn't turned to watch. I slid out the wheel, made sure the gun was fully loaded, then scooped up a handful of loose bullets from the drawer and stuffed them in my shirt pocket. I spun the wheel and clicked it back in place. I laughed to myself as I gripped the pistol in my left hand, looking at the back of Sam's head. Poor kid was so into his game he was completely oblivious to his surroundings. I could have been some madman standing behind him. Some kind of crazy bastard just wishing for the opportunity to blow the back of some kid's head off. I pointed the gun in his general direction, stuck my tongue out and shut one eye.

His mother made a noise in the front room and I had just enough time to slip the revolver back into its case before Sam turned his head toward the door. He cocked his head to the side before returning to his game. The look on his face was that of utter boredom.

How could he be so damned bored and at the same time even be thinking about playing through forty two levels of a video game? Why would he commit to something like that when it didn't seem whatsoever exciting to him? Kid was a damn weirdo.

I put the gun case away, grabbed a light leather jacket from the closet and left the room.

I was heading for the door when my cell phone rang. I almost tripped over Maggie's legs retrieving it from where I'd left it on the couch. I did not recognize the number on the screen and hesitated to answer it. I let it ring several times, staring at the number and imagining everybody it could be I was terrified to speak with. I grit my teeth and looked at Maggie. It seemed like anybody that could be calling would be calling because of her, if not for her. Who the hell wanted to talk to me? As long as it wasn't-

I answered it.

"--Yo, Frank--"

I hung up, flipping the phone shut. Then I laughed. I had so much expected it to be someone I didn't want to speak to, that I'd instinctively hung up on Mitch. Maggie looked up at me with a questioning look. "Who was it?" she asked.

"Don't worry about it," I said, making myself serious.

I re-opened the phone and scrolled through the received calls, found the number Mitch had used and called back.

"Mitch, hey! Hey! What's up?" I practically shouted. I could feel my excitement vibrating in my solar plexus. He'd changed his mind. I knew it. Of course he hadn't really meant to fire me. Mitch knew a winner when he had one.

"Frankie boy," said Mitch, sounding like the old father figure I'd always thought of him as. "The Frankster."

"Yeah. Yeah, Mitch. What's going on? I didn't recognize the number."

"Yeah, I know," he wheezed. "Figured you wouldn't answer my call, so I borrowed Lonnie's phone." Lonnie, the under 21, oversexed waitress Mitch hired six months earlier, for the exact reason any man hires an under 21, oversexed wannabe waitress. I made a mental note. I had her phone number now.

"Yeah. Uh-huh," I said, confused. "Why wouldn't I answer your call, Mitch?"

Mitch breathed a sigh, paused. "Well, Frank. I guess I figured you're still pretty sore with me. Maybe you don't wanna speak to ol' Mitch."

"That's ridiculous, man. Why wouldn't I want to talk--?"

"Here's why I'm calling, Frank--"

"Uh-huh?"

"Well, you left your guitar in my office. It's kinda nice, you know, so I thought you'd like to know it's here."

"Sure."

Another pause from Mitch. "So, yeah. You think

you might want to come and get it, or should I have it brought out to you?"

"Uh-huh. Yeah."

"Well, ah… which is it? Hey, you okay there, Frankie boy?"

"Ahem… hmm. Ah-huh. Well, Mitch. I think you've probably got a final paycheck of mine floating around that office, too."

"Aw, Frank. You know I'm gonna have to let the bookkeeper…"

I hung up.

Again, I regretted my inability to speak my mind. It's not so much that I'm a nice person. I just can't stand for anybody not to like me. You might be thinking maybe there's no difference and, hey, what do I know. And, yeah, I guess most people are only nice for a reason. But with me, it's like being on the telephone with your grandmother. It's never a very pleasant conversation, but you can't bring yourself to hang up on her. That exact feeling has been my problem in life, my entire life. Whatever it was, at least as long as I wanted my job back, I needed for Mitch to like me being around. I don't think that's so hard to understand.

I gazed once more at Maggie in her mellowed out state. I thought about saying something to her, but couldn't think of a single word. I made sure to lock the door as I left. I won't go into it yet, what happened later that night. It's still a little hazy in my mind, and I wouldn't like to give you any unclear details. It just wouldn't be fair. One thing that is clear, though, vividly, audibly clear… and just imagine this… a Bossa Nova beat.

# CHAPTER 5

I STOOD OVER the kitchen sink washing the blood from my hands. I kept the water pressure low so as not to wake Maggie and the boy. That seemed to give the streaks and spots of blood on my wrists more time to congeal and crust up. I scraped at it with my fingernails, pulling out arm hairs and shivering at the thought of digging microscopic trenches into my flesh for the blood to smear into. I held my hands up to the dim light over the stove to make sure I'd gotten all the blood off, then wiped them dry on my pants leg. I turned the water off and stopped the sink, then poured in about two cups of bleach and let it sit.

I opened the window above the sink a crack to keep the bleach smell from filling the room. I never could stand the smell of bleach. It's not that it's toxic, because I don't mind the smell of gasoline or motor oil. I think it's because bleach smells like sperm a little... kind of. Give it a whiff sometime, you'll see. It's not just me, buddy. But, yeah. I guess I don't like the smell of sperm either. Not sure if it's because it smells like bleach or not. What came first, the chicken or the egg, right? Ah... I don't know. It bugs me that it bugs me, you know?

I let the bleach sit for a few minutes then pulled the drain plug. I wasn't even for sure if it made a difference, but I didn't want no blood crusting up in my pipes. And yeah, I guess it was just a bit of paranoia. But better to be safe than sorry. And hey, I wasn't even sure if I had a right to be worried in the first place. Most likely I was being oversensitive. Just like most times. I hadn't really done anything wrong. Not in the biblical sense. Or the, uh. I mean a guy can't help an accident, right? That's why they're called accidents.

I went to the bathroom, walking softly, keeping quiet, and sat down to urinate. I finished, washed my hands again- this time with soap, and checked myself in the mirror. I gave a satisfactory nod. I'd always known I was a good looking guy. Figured it out in... say, junior high. But it wasn't till the last couple years I came to really appreciate it. Now, I never used it to no advantage or anything, but I think I could, if I wanted to. And I did derive a certain satisfaction from it. I leaned in to the mirror, close. Squeezed a few blackheads from my nose, then smoothed out my sideburns. Yeah, I guess I looked a little like Elvis. Just then, there was a movement behind me. Startled, I banged my head against the mirror.

"Jesus Christ, Maggie. The bathroom's occupied."

Maggie didn't say anything. Her eyes weren't even opened. But she nodded kind of absently as she dropped her underwear and sat down on the toilet. I stepped back, leaned against the sink and stared at her naked thighs.

"Maggie," I said, snapping my fingers next to her face. She didn't respond. Sleepwalking, I guessed. If there was such a thing.

*Sleepwalking? Come on, man.*

My eyes took her in. And I mean all of her. Her perfectly shaped toes, just the right length, only slightly covered by her panties. Her soft white feet, scuffed up and a little dirty from walking around the house barefoot. My eyes slithered over and up her legs like a snake all the way to what I'd wanted to see from the moment I first met her. It was hiding just a little bit in the shadow thrown from her upper body, but I could see the hairline well enough, and a little bit of her... little thingy peeking out. She leaned her head back a little, stretched and yawned, but her eyes remained closed.

I crept forward slowly and waved my hand in front of her face. I whispered, "Maggie." But again, nothing. She moaned like as if she were having a dream, and slumped over, propping her elbows on her thighs.

I chuckled. I don't know. It was funny in a way. I'd never seen anybody sleepwalk before. I wondered if I'd ever walked in my sleep. Lord knows there were times I got up late in the night to take a piss, without knowing any better until seeing it in the toilet bowl the next morning.

I reached out and touched the bottom half of her nightshirt, rubbed it between my fingers. It was just a regular nightshirt. 100 percent cotton. But it felt like a winning fucking lottery ticket. I lifted it slowly, raising it from the back so I could see the curve of her ass. I peered around behind her for a better view, admiring her lower back and the dimples above her ass cheeks. I looked to see if she'd opened her eyes yet. Nope.

Was she really sleepwalking, or was this her way of inviting me to make a move without really putting herself on the line. If I wanted to do something, great. If not, she could use the sleepwalking as an excuse. After all, she'd been sitting there for almost a minute and hadn't urinated yet. It was as much an invitation as anything.

*What the hell.*

I unzipped my fly and pulled myself out. I grabbed the shaft of my penis at the base and squeezed. I was so excited I could cum right then and there, and I didn't want that to happen. Not yet. I didn't want to waste it. I held it out in front of her face, feeling my heart race and the pulse in the head of my penis, and I, sort of hesitantly, pointed the tip towards her slightly opened mouth. There was a little dribble of spit at the side of her mouth and I focused on that. I felt like I was going to faint I was breathing so hard. She was right there. Her mouth was right there! And… and then she started to urinate.

I caught and held my breath as the slow trickle became a torrent, echoing off the bathroom walls, loud as Niagara Falls. As quickly as I could, I tucked myself back in and zipped up. Like a slug, I slunk out of the bathroom as quickly and quietly as I could, and plopped down on the couch. A few seconds later Maggie shuffled out of the bathroom and back to the bedroom. She hadn't flushed the toilet. I elbowed the couch cushions and my pillow, then jumped up, went back to the bathroom and gave it a flush. Then I sat down to masturbate. I started out thinking of the last several minutes, thinking about her body, then went on fantasizing about what I had hoped would happen and all the things I could have done with her. Things I'd always fantasized about before. Then my mind went back to way earlier in the night, before I had come home. I recalled the blood on my hands and how it had got there. And... and that worked too.

Don't go thinking I'm depraved, or anything like that. You have to admit it was an easy situation to be confused by. Exciting and arousing... both. And God knows I hadn't had too much to be excited or aroused by for a while. I know what you're thinking now. In a town built on vice, filled with showgirls, exotic dancers, and dial-a-prostitutes, this guy can't get excited or aroused? But, yeah, man. Dang if I can't help it when the word *female* becomes synonymous with disease. If I didn't care about my health and, yeah, have a little bit of self-respect, I wouldn't need to masturbate. If anything, I'm not depraved enough. Goddamn it. What are we, in high school, here?

After that, I lay back down on the couch and fell asleep. I was out for a good five or six hours when I was awoken by the beep-boop-beepedy damn noise of Sam's damn video game. I opened my eyes as little as possible and saw him crouched on the floor, leaning against the armrest of the couch, his head right under my feet. I lifted my head, which took some strength, tired as I was, and tried to see what time the clock on the wall had. My eyes were too blurry from sleep to tell. My head fell back on the pillow as if it weighed a hundred pounds. I yawned and stretched and growled.

"It's goddamn scary how you're always playing with that thing, man," I said to Sam, covering my face with my forearm. Of course he had no reply. "Why are you out here anyway? You can't play that thing in the bedroom? It's loud."

"I didn't want to wake mom up."

"So you wake me up?"

He shrugged. "This is the living room."

"Oh, come on." I swung my feet over his head and hopped off the couch. I stomped to the kitchen and opened the refrigerator door hoping to God the bacon was still good. It was. I tossed the package of bacon on the counter, reached back in for the orange juice and loaf of bread then slammed the door back shut. "You know better than that, kid. Don't act like a jerk. I let you and your mom have my bedroom so the both of you can sleep better, and you don't even think about helping me out by being a little quieter while I'm sleeping- out here- for you." I turned the front burner of the stove to medium low, lay ten slices of bacon in a pan and placed the pan on the burner. I dropped two slices of bread into the toaster and poured orange juice into two glasses. "Hey, man, I know you're probably not the happiest kid on earth right now. You're away from home and you got no friends here and who knows what's going on with your mom and dad, but try and have just a little bit of respect for me, alright. You hear what I'm saying?" No reply. My head just shook. "You want some breakfast?"

"Um- hum," he mumbled, I guess in the affirmative, and I handed him a glass of orange juice. I readjusted the couch cushions and sat down so I could watch him play the game. I rubbed my eyes. It was hard to tell what was on the screen from what my own blurry vision saw. "Jesus," I groaned. "Hey can you pause that or something?"

"Why?"

"Because I need you to go back in my room and get me some fresh socks."

"Why can't you do it?"

Little mother fucker.

"Because… your mom's in there."

"Yeah, but she's sleeping."

"She might have woke up. She might be in there half naked, getting changed or something."

"Well, I don't want to see that."

"Why would that bother you? Okay, yeah. I guess you wouldn't want to see that. Well, look. Just knock first."

"But that will wake her up if she isn't awake."

"Fuck cares. Go get my socks."

"Fine." He paused the game. The pink gorilla was frozen, hovering over what looked like a giant Venus fly trap. "I'm not getting you underwear."

"I didn't ask for underwear, did I?"

Sam placed the game down on the coffee table and jumped over my feet on the way to the bedroom. I could have tripped him but I didn't. I waited until he was out of sight before grabbing the game. I let my index finger hover over it, looking for the pause button. Finding it, I un-paused the game until the pink gorilla was swallowed by one of the Venus flytrap thingy's, then re-paused it and put the game back         where         he'd         left         it.

He came back and tossed my socks at my feet, then let out a big sigh. "She's still sleeping," he said.

I smelled the socks before putting them on. "So what? She's tired."

Sam bent to pick up his game, looked at the screen and slumped. He put the game back on the table and pushed it slowly away from him. "That's not funny," he said.

I grinned. Obviously, I found it entirely funny. It had been the quickest, easiest way to lash out at the little shit. I couldn't very well slap him across the face now, could I? Could I?

The bacon was sizzling, and I got up to turn off the burner. "How many pieces do you want?" I asked.

"Is it crispy?"

That merited a snort. "Ain't this America?"

"Three, then, please," he said.

"Okay. Three. Now we're getting somewhere," I said. I took the bread from the toaster, covered each slice with butter and laid the bacon next to them. When I looked up, Sam was sitting at the kitchen table. I sighed and brought him the plate. Little bastard had probably been conditioned from birth to eat every meal at the kitchen table. It was most likely Maggie's one single accomplishment in child rearing, and the closest she'd ever come to building a functioning household. I guessed I'd have to eat at the table too while the kid was around, for fear of destroying what little she *had* built. I may not give much of a damn, but I'm not quite cocksucker enough to do that to her.

I watched Sam eat. He had a peculiar way of devouring the bacon strips. He ate them almost like a corn on the cob. Holding the bacon at both ends and whittling away at it with his teeth, in tiny little bites. It was fascinating in a way. Almost abnormal. I began to wonder if Sam had Asperger's Syndrome or something like it, the way he could concentrate so much on one little thing. Especially for a kid addicted to video games. I watched him eat the way I would watch an animal in the zoo. A thought was striking me. I couldn't quite put my finger on it, but it had something to do with the eccentricities of ingestion, and... and stuff like that... and. Then I thought of last night and the look on Lonnie Higgins' face when I--. He finished his first bacon slice, picked up another and looked at me, with grease smeared across his face. He began to wipe his hands on his pants, paused, waited to see if I was going to say anything... then kept on until his pants were stained dark with bacon fat. I wondered what his momma would say about that. Wondered what his dad would say. His dad with half his fingers missing. I wondered what the mother fucker's hand looked like. I visualized it in my head. The stubs, all stitched up, swollen and red... the rest of the hand aged and brown... the remaining fingers dangling loosely, appearing elongated and alien...

"E-yuck," said Sam. "Your nose is bleeding all over the place."

I looked down as a drop of blood dripped down to a small pool forming in the cavity of my hand between my thumb and forefinger. It was already overflowing, dripping and drying and running in darker, coagulating stains across my palm and wrist. I sniffed and leaned my head back. The coppery tang of blood ran down my throat and, for a brief second I was close to panic. "Aw, hell," I moaned.

I tore some paper towels off the roll and leaned over the sink. I ran the water and splashed my face a couple times before wiping the blood off my hand. Curiously, it took a bit more effort to wash away the blood from my nose than it had the blood from... well, from my accident with Lonnie Higgins. I'll go ahead and say it.

I rolled up two small pieces of paper towel and stuffed them in my nostrils, dried my hands and rejoined Sam at the table. He stared at me with what I can only assume was a mixture of disgust and the child's natural desire to make fun. I stared right back at him. Deadly serious. Without even a blink.

It went on like this for... maybe a whole minute.

Sam sighed, then, and finished his breakfast. "Don't you have work, or something?" he asked.

I leaned back and crossed my arms. *Well, ain't this little kid a son of a bitch?* Trying to run me out of my own house.

"What's it to you?"

A shrug, his head down. "Nothing."

"Well, if it ain't nothing to you, why are you asking?"

"That's what grown-up's do, right? You go to work. You have a job, don't you?"

I felt my chest cave in just a bit. He was right. What kind of a man was I? Walking around without

a job.  How was I going to pay the rent?  The bills?
How soon before I became a welfare slut like all the
Spico's and Indians and Katrina refugees?  I was
worse than shit.  Worse than dog shit.  God Almighty!

"Just shows what you know, kid," I said, removing
the tissue balls from my nostrils.  They were soaked
red, about halfway through, but my nose had stopped
bleeding.  "I got better than a job.  I play the guitar
for a living."

"Nuh-uh."

"Yeah."

"Whatever.  That's not a job.  Are you any good?"

I stared blankly.  "Am I any good?  Well… let me
put it to you this way.  You've heard of Elvis
Pressley?"

Sam stared at the ceiling, squinted.  "Um…?"

"Jailhouse Rock.  Heartbreak Hotel."

"…"

"Blue Suede Shoes.  Teddy Bear."

"…"

"Good Luck Charm.  Love Me Tender.  God
Damn!"

"Ha-ha!  Just kidding.  I've heard of him."

I breathed a sigh of relief.  "Whew.  Kid, I thought I
was going to have to slap your mom for a minute
there."  I chuckled and shook my head, but then saw
Sam's eyes had grown wide, and realized I'd maybe
crossed a line with him.  I guess you really can't joke
with a kid about hurting his mother.  Especially when
his father made a habit out of it.  And look what
happened there.  "Ahem… well, yeah well, you know
Elvis Presley was the King, right?  And I can play just

about everything he ever played, so I guess that makes me pretty good, then, doesn't it?"

"Hmm." He nodded softly and looked down at the floor again. "How come I never heard you on the radio then?"

"Well, now, the radio isn't all where it's at. Especially in a town like this that we're in now." I waved my hands in the air. "No, sir. You have to play in front of people if you want to be anything. You have to have an audience."

Sam looked around. I could see it in his face he was still skeptical. "If you play the guitar, how come I don't see a single guitar in your house?"

"That's because... that's because..." my words stumbled against each other. "I left my guitar at... where I work. One of my work places. It was... uh. On accident."

Sam giggled. "Geez. Calm down. I was only asking."

I leaned forward. Suddenly I couldn't take my eyes off of the front door. I stared at the knob and imagined it slowly turning. Vibrating slightly, as if someone were trying to get in. Almost every dream I've ever woken up from ends with something banging on a door.

"Huh. You know, it's funny, Sam," I said, quietly. "When I left the house last night. That's what I went to do. To pick up my guitar. But I don't... uh, I guess I didn't."

Sam just stared at me. It didn't mean anything to him.

"It's weird. Isn't it?"

He didn't say anything and I didn't say anything else. We both leaned to peer down the hall, and if the two of us ever had anything in common it was the desire for his mother to come out of the bedroom right at that moment, just to break up the silence. So, yeah, we just sat there, the both of us. Just sat at the table doing nothing and talking about nothing. It was uncomfortable as all hell. And there was really no need for it. I even chuckled a little bit about it. It was like some strange oppressive force had laid down over me. And for whatever reason I was stuck at that table because I was afraid it would hurt the kid's feelings if I got up and walked away from him. That was it, really. It's one of the reasons I don't like having company. It's one of the reasons I don't have very many friends. I'm deeply afraid of hurting anybody's feelings. Sincerely.

I let my eyes drift to the digital clock sitting on top of the refrigerator. We had been sitting in silence for five minutes. It felt like an eternity. Jesus Christ. It was getting hard to breathe. There were a million things I could do. I'd been in similar spots before, and I'd learned to think retrospectively, to put things in perspective, in order not to feel out of my depth. I could say I had to use the restroom. I could get up and make coffee. I could go outside and check the mail. But I didn't.

That's the problem with guys like me, you see? We get overwhelmed for some reason, by very insignificant things. Or, at least they seem insignificant in retrospect, and certainly to other people.

I lit a cigarette and steadied my eyes on Sam. I could reach across the table and jab my hand into his throat. If I did that, I could break the monotony. I could get up and go about my day. I could grab a handful of his hair and bash his head against the table until his skull split open. It seemed... almost easier than sitting in silence. If I did it real quickly like, he wouldn't have time to be upset at me, or sad about it. And it probably wouldn't hurt him much, if at all.

My breath caught in my chest. I shook my head, knowing none of the discomfort showed on my face. I almost wish it had.

"So what did you do last night?"

"Huh? What?"

"You said you went out last night to get your guitar, but you didn't. So what did you do?"

"Hah. I don't... I don't know. Did I say that?"

"What?"

"That I went to get my guitar last night?"

"Yeah. You said it was weird. And then you started blowing your nasty cigarette smoke in my face."

I stood up then, and stuffed my hands in my pockets. I took a long drag on the cigarette, burning the cherry to a long stem. I felt my lungs fill, and my stomach go a little bit queasy. I exhaled. Watched the smoke get caught in the filthy orange light shade dangling over the kitchen table. It circled it like water in a bucket before dissipating completely. Then I crossed over to Sam and tousled his hair before jabbing the cigarette out in the sink.

I leaned against the counter. "You ever say things

you never meant to say?"

"I don't know," Sam replied, smoothing his hair back down. "You mean like telling a lie?"

"Eh…" I lit another cigarette. "Nah, I don't mean like a lie. I mean, like, well… like me telling you about the guitar. You know, I don't know why I'd tell you something like that. Not that I mind you knowing about it. That's alright. That's no big deal. I just hate that it slipped out like that. You know? It just flew right outta my mouth. Now suppose that had been something important. Supposing I had a secret. A deep, deep secret. How do I know I won't just blurt it out one of these days?"

"Maybe you shouldn't have secrets."

"Oh, but come on now, Sam. Everybody has secrets. You can't get through life without having at least one. They just kind of grow on you. Like… like the rings of a tree." I took a few quick puffs of the cigarette to get a better burn, inhaled and exhaled. "What are you, Sam? You're like nine years old now, right? I'll bet you've already got a few secrets, yourself."

Sam hunched down. Sort of looked like he was trying to dip his head into his chest, like a turtle retreating into its shell.

"Yeah, I knew it," I gloated, smiling. "Everybody's got one. I told you."

"Well," he hesitated. "I guess maybe I do have one."

I turned a chair around and sat back down. "Come on. Let's hear it."

"If I tell you, it won't be a secret anymore."

"Yeah. Right. Exactly. You don't want secrets, kid. You hold onto them too long, they shrivel you up inside. That's why old folks look so messed up. Because of all the secrets they've picked up over the years."

"I guess," he said, still hesitating.

I sighed. "All right, kid. Even trade. What do you want?"

His eyes sparkled. "I want to go somewhere. I'm tired of sitting here cooped up in your house."

"Ha! Okay. You got it," I said, slapping my knees. "You let loose of that secret and I'll take you into town with me."

"You mean it?"

"Shit yeah. I mean it."

"Mom called Aunt Mary-Anne and told her we were staying here."

"She did…," I shook my head. "Say what?"

"That's my secret."

"That is… --about. Your mom calling her sister is your secret?"

"Well. Mom told me not to tell you because she knew it would make you mad."

*You can choke a bitch out pretty quick with a sports sock… nobody has a good choke threshold. Forget all the S&M bullshit. It'll be over almost as soon as you get your hands…*

"What makes her- uh, think that'll, that that will make me--." I took a deep, long breath of air, and exhaled loudly. "What did she…? She didn't talk about me at all, or anything, right? She didn't tell your Aunt anything about how I'm living, or anything *at all* about me, did she Sam? She didn't say - *anything*--- about me. Other than that you guys are staying here?"

Sam looked like he was about to cringe. Had he been a little older and a little wiser, he might have. "No. I don't think so."

"Whew. Ha-ha!" I faked a laugh. "Yeah that was a close…ah. That's good, she didn't. That's real good. It's good you told me, kid. That wasn't, uh… that wasn't fair of your mother to ask you to keep that from me. But that's okay. That's okay. As long as there's… no harm done, then… no harm no foul. It's not really fair… it's kind of un-cool that your mom would call that cu--, your Aunt, from my… from my home. But it's… it is understandable."

"So… you're not mad at her, are you?"

"Uh… which one?"

"My mom."

"Your mom? Aw, heck no. No. N-no. Naw. Naw. Naw. I ain't mad at her, kid. It's just that I ain't exactly on good terms with your Aunt. And I'd sure hate for… well, let's just leave it alone. Okay?"

He shrugged again. It's all so simple for them. "Sure," he chirped.

"Just so long as she used her own cell phone," I continued. "You know what I'm saying? She did use her own phone, right? Because I wouldn't want your Aunt to get hold of my phone number. You know, I mean, it's not absolutely necessary having a landline these days, but I do enjoy having it."

"No. She used her cell. But it's really not that hard to find somebody's number. Phones are like fingerprints these days. And landlines are the worst. I didn't even know people still had them. Not regular people anyways. For their house."

"Well, Sam. I find that it is possible to make time slow down when you oppose change. You can never underestimate a creature of habit. I'm like a… like a god damn… tortoise, man."

Sam looked around the living room, giving the stink-eye to every piece of outdated, obsolete machinery in the place, then threw up his hands. "In your case, I would say so," he said. "Is that a VCR?"

That's about when the phone rang. The big 'ol corded telephone hooked to the land line. Yeah. The land line. I ignored the look on Sam's face as I went to answer it. I don't think he even knew what it was.

"Hello," I spat into the receiver, feeling, for the first time, embarrassed about the telephone.

"Hey there, Frank," came Mitch's tired drawl.

*Eee-yuh…*

"Hello, yourself, Mitch," I said, nice and even as can be. But really, I was thinking to myself, how is this son of a bitch taking the time to call me after what I did last night? Shouldn't he have more pressing matters to deal with? Something else to be concerned about? I checked the time.

"I sure don't want to keep bugging you about this, Frank. But your guitar is just taking up a whole lot of space in my office and I'd hate to have it thrown out."

"You sound downright concerned about it, Mitch," I said. *For a mutt bastard alright. You're lucky you're still breathing.* "But don't you worry none. I'm coming to get it right now. Matter of fact, I'm out the door already."

I hung up, sighed and said to Sam. "Write your mom a note, kid. Let's go to town. Come on, giddy-up."

# CHAPTER 6

MITCH GAVE ME one of his stupid looks when I walked into his office. He had about a dozen of them. Stupid looks, I mean. His left eyebrow was cocked and his upper lip rose at one side in what was supposed to be a grin, but it looked more like he was about to start making fart noises with his mouth. Asshole is just in some peoples genes. I may have said that already. But it's true. That's why it's written all over their faces. Hard to believe I ever liked the son of a bitch. He leaned back in his chair, reached behind him and scratched at my guitar with his finger. Someone had set it inside a plain black guitar case, I guess to be nice.

"You come for this?" he asked.

"Yep."

"This one right here. This here guitar?"

"Heh- heh. That's the one. Yessir."

"Well now," Mitch rubbed his chin. "You got any proof this here guitar is yours? I wouldn't want to just give it away to some… strange person."

"Come on now, Mitch," I said, shaking my head.

Mitch howled a high pitched laugh, emptying his god damn lungs, and clapped his hands together. "Shit man. Sit down already, will ya. You make me nervous standing there like that."

"Well I ain't really got the time," I said, jerking my thumb toward the door. "I got somebody waiting."

I'd left Sam at the bar. He was tucked in between two burnt out old barfly's and sipping on a root beer. I knew Mona, the lady behind the bar, and I figured she'd look after him. She even flipped the television over the bar to one of the kiddy channels for him. Most of these people ain't all bad. Mostly the only bad thing about them is they're ugly as shit. I don't know. Maybe it's from watching too many movies as a kid, but, ugly ass people just always seemed to me to be like... well, not exactly evil-- but, well... kinda painted that color. You know?

Mitch gestured pathetically to the chair in front of his desk. I sighed, lit a cigarette and sat down.

"All serious now," he said. "I guess you ain't coming back to work the line?"

I took a long drag on the cigarette. The ceiling of Mitch's office was real low, maybe just seven feet, and I always liked the way that closeness made a cigarette taste. It reminded me of smoking my first cigarettes in the bathroom stalls way back in junior high. I exhaled. "What are you talking about?" I asked.

"Well, you know, just so's you understand, but just because I don't want you playing up on stage... it don't mean I wanted you fired or nothing. You can still... I mean, I wasn't trying to get rid of you in the kitchen."

I sniffed. Kind of clicked my tongue in my mouth and ashed my cigarette. "That just don't make a whole hell of a lot of sense now does it, Mitch?" I asked.

I waited for him to elaborate a little on what he was

trying to say, but he just sat there and stared at me with his hands far apart like he was waiting to catch something falling out of the sky. He blinked rapidly and shook his head, then said, "Well, whatever, Frank. I just wanted to make that clear to you. But I understand. I guess I understand."

"You think I was put on this earth to make grilled cheese?" I asked, maybe a little too quickly, because it seemed to startle him. "You telling me the whole entire time we've known each other, you think I was more important as a griddle cook than as an entertainer?"

He waved his hands in the air. "No. No. But the one thing was your job, and the other was just something I let you do for fun. To fill the air. And I'm not saying you weren't any good," he said, adding slowly, "But it wasn't serious, Frank. It was supposed to be like… like a novelty. You just took it too serious."

"Can I have my guitar now?"

"Well, yeah. Yeah. There's just…" He swiveled in his chair, turned around and picked up my guitar case, then swiveled back around and set it on top of his desk. He wasn't wearing one of his stupid looks now. I wanted to reach across the desk and smack him. I felt my face getting hot and knew I was getting red and that embarrassed me a little. It embarrassed me that I was upset. It was embarrassing that he could tell I was upset. Guys like Mitch are part of the reason I don't like to step out of doors. Less than five minutes in his office and he had me feeling small and pathetic. And with his bullshit stories, it was enough to make other people think I was small and pathetic. When people are always making you feel small, you start to thinking you're a prick for just believing in yourself. He'd heard me play. He'd seen the crowd react. But to him I was like… almost like just a burger flipper, or something. You believe that shit?

"I wanted to talk to you about-," he kept on, leaned in close and lowered his voice. "Did you hear what happened last night?"

I lit another cigarette with the butt end of the old cigarette and tossed the butt into the ash tray on Mitch's desk. I crossed one leg over the other, bounced my foot in the air and stared directly at the face of the clock on the wall. "Well, I don't know," I said with a drawl. "I guess about a million things might've happened last night. I may have heard about one or two of them."

Mitch made as if to look out his door into the hallway, but there was nothing to see out there but the brick wall outside his office. Every now and then a straggler would waltz by in search of a bathroom, but you could hear them shimmy down the hall a ways before they reached the door. I tapped my foot on the floor, listened to it echo off the cold, grey walls. Mitch cleared his throat and gestured with his hand. "Can I bum a smoke?" he asked, holding his hand up with two fingers out, as if the fingers required a cigarette to fill the void.

I popped one out of the pack and tossed it over to him. He missed it in the air and it landed and rolled on his desk. He caught it before it rolled to the floor and brought it up to his mouth with another of those stupid ass looks. He declined my box of matches and used a nice butane lighter of his own. He took a long drag then cleared his throat again. "It was, ah… you remember Lonnie. Lonnie Higgins? The waitress girl. Part timer. Real pretty."

I continued tapping my foot on the floor and nodded slowly, smiled. "Yeah. Yeah. You called me from her phone last night, remember?" I took my phone from my pocket, flipped it open and scrolled through it.

"Yep. I remember asking about where you were calling from on account of the out of state area code." I filled my lungs with smoke and brought my lower lip down in a sort of ignorant frown. "I guess she hasn't bothered to change that yet. But it was something I noticed."

Mitch stretched his hands out then brought them back in and crossed his arms over his chest. "Yeah, yeah, yeah, yeah," he muttered, shaking his head. "Yeah, I guess you haven't heard."

"I guess not."

"Well, hell. Why would you have heard anything, right?" He gave a short laugh, and said, "Well, anyway… anyway. Looks like she got herself beat half to death. She's in the hospital right now. You believe that?"

"Lonnie Higgins?"

"Yeah. Yeah. Can you believe it? And I was with her last night, too. The Police were in here first thing this morning asking all sorts of questions. That's why I'm so out of it, man. Shit, man, it felt like an IRS audit. Those boys sure know how to make a person sweat."

"Um-hum," I kept on nodding, chewing my lower lip. "They know who did it?"

Mitch shrugged slightly. "I don't suppose so. Guessing by some of the questions they was asking, I don't think they got too many ideas, either. I guess Lonnie wasn't much help, herself. Barbara went down to see her in the hospital this morning, soon as the cops left. Said there ain't no tubes stuck in her or anything, but I guess it looks like her face got ran over by a milk truck. I guess she's been pretty out of it since it happened. And you know, cops probably want to wait until she's well enough before they start prodding her for anything."

He bent down to reach into the bottom drawer and came back up with a pint bottle of Jack. He took a couple pulls, wiped his mouth and made another look. "It's kind of sad, really. She was a nice girl."

"Oh, I don't know, Mitch. I'm sure she's *still* really nice," I said. "Unless she's learned some kind of lesson."

Mitch stared at me with a kind of confused look, and I laughed to let him know I was probably joking. He took another pull from the bottle then put it back in the drawer. I reached into my jacket pocket and fondled the underwear I'd snatched from Lonnie's apartment. I bunched it up in my fist and scuffed my shoe against the leg of his desk. I raised my eyes to about Mitch's jaw line and asked, "So the cops know you were with her then."

He cleared his throat, tried to pass it off as a belch,

and sniffed. "Yeah. Yep. I mean, I guess that was one of the main reasons they came by here this morning. But, like I said, I didn't have anything for them. Not much anyway. I mean, now they know it happened sometime after ten o'clock because that's when I left her. And I know it wasn't me who bust her up."

"You think the cops believe you?"

"Well, why shouldn't they?" he asked, but his eyes got a little bit watery. He stuck his hands out, knuckles up. "These look like hands that just beat the shit outta somebody? Hell."

I quickly looked down at my own hands. They were both fine, except for a scrape on the pinky knuckle of my left hand. But that could have been from anything. I wasn't too concerned about that. I was more concerned about how I hadn't thought of that at all. If both my hands had been swollen to twice their normal size, I would have walked right into Mitch's office like it was nothing. Except for my socks, I was wearing the same clothes.

*Fuck.*

"Uhgn," I grunted.

"Huh. What?"

"Nothing," I said. "It's just really too bad. Senseless like." I shook my head. "It's a messed up world."

"Ain't it though," Mitch shook his head along with me. "Know what's really sad? That girl was clean too. A real good girl. No messing about. And some scum sucker has to go and have his way with her."

I sat up. "What do you mean?"

"You know, Frank," he leaned in again and whispered, like he was afraid of what he was saying, "Raped."

My jaw dropped. "What makes you think she was raped?"

"Well, shit. Who beats a woman half to death without raping her?"

I sucked air through my teeth and clenched my fingers around the armrests of my chair, thinking about swinging it on top of his head.

He went on. "I know. I know. Makes you mad, don't it? I mean... you know this kind of shit happens, but man, not to someone you know. I mean *know*- know. Right?"

"Did the Police say she was raped?" I asked, trying to keep my voice from cracking. "How would they know that if she can't even speak to them? Maybe it was another *girl* that beat the shit out of her. A girl ain't going to rape nobody."

"Nah. Nah. Well, maybe. What do I know? Maybe she wasn't all the way raped or anything like that. But apparently her titties were all messed up. One of 'em practically torn off. That's what Barbara said, at least."

I was getting sort of nauseous. Just the idea of it. What a bunch of presumptuous sons of bitches. They took a few scrapes and bruises and blew it all out of proportion. All of a sudden it's a conspiracy. All of a sudden she was raped. It just pops into their minds. Some police. Some professionals. Bunch of fucking dingbats, I say. Maybe they're the sickos. Maybe they're the perverts. For just having it on their minds so much, right? For just having it there, ready to pull out of thin air. And, god damn, what kind of a world is this we live in that a beaten woman is raped so god damn often, it's automatically assumed she's going to be violated every time someone busts her face up? And just like that sweet little Lonnie's transformed into some kind of wayward angel.

*Fuck.*

It wouldn't happen in a world where men took care of women. Where men defended women. Where women didn't run around, wearing practically nothing at all as if in defiance of men. Fucking daring them. But really, if women would just recognize their place as the weaker of the species, maybe we as a society could curb the amount of sexual assault. Maybe. Just maybe. And we shouldn't use the word 'weaker'. I shouldn't have used the word 'weaker'. We should say 'delicate'. Delicate should be what women allow themselves to be. And then, maybe when they got attacked, it wouldn't be to take ownership of some sexuality that was... well, let's face it, flaunted in the first place; but instead, it would be from a simple, almost imperceptible desire to crush something 'delicate'. Like tearing the wings off a dragonfly, or lopping the head off a flower. The motives of the attack would be simpler. Clearer. More easily investigated, solved, or prevented.

"Jeez," I said, shaking my head at Mitch. "You don't seem all that broken up about it. Doesn't it bother you? I mean, you were with her maybe... maybe just seconds before it happened."

"Life in the Big City," he shrugged, nonchalant like.

I stared at him for a while. I had to pick up my jaw several times as my mouth kept falling open. "Damn, Mitch. That's harsh."

"Now don't get me wrong," he said, bobbing his head. "I'm not trying to come off heartless. I feel bad for the girl, but it's hardly the end of the world. I mean, come on. Really. Whether I was with her seconds before or hours before doesn't really make a difference. It's not like I can put it in some kind of… personal context. Like, uh… like, it could have been me, or something? I guess, yeah, possibly it wouldn't have happened if I stuck around. But I couldn't be there all the time. It's not like we were involved with anything serious, right? And let's get real here, Frank. There's a reason I wasn't there, and that's because she wouldn't put out. She didn't want to put out so I beat it. So I can't really think that way, now, can I, about… why… why I wasn't there? I mean, seriously, if I had been there, who's gonna rape me instead of Lonnie?"

"Stop saying that. You don't know for sure she was raped," I tried to control my voice, pinching myself just under my ribs. "That could be a bunch of horseshit. Could be… could… probably is horseshit. But whoever beat her half to death… maybe, could maybe beat you half to death. So maybe… maybe it could have been you instead of her."

Mitch sat back and shook his head. A ridiculous smirk on his lips. "Nah. Nah," he said. "I don't think so."

"You don't think so?"

"Nah," he repeated. "First of all, I'm not a 105

pound woman. And second. Uh... uh... uh... it's just, it's just stupid to even think about it."

I leaned my head back, looked at the ceiling, then pinched my eyes shut and sighed. "Yeah. You're right. It's stupid to think about."

"Jesus. You'd think you had something going with the girl."

"No. I just... I feel bad. Stuff like this always brings me down. She's someone's daughter, and sister, and shit, you know?"

"Yeah," Mitch mumbled. "I guess that's why I brought it up to you. Not to bring you down. But, I guess I needed someone other than a cop to talk about it with."

"Uh-huh."

It got quiet for a couple minutes. I kept my eyes to the floor and he kept his on his desk. My chair creaked a few times when my weight shifted and he looked up then, expecting me to get up and leave. I knew that's what he was waiting for. For me to get up and take myself and my guitar out of his office. But I knew Mitch. Probably even better than he knew himself. Or, at least better than he wanted people to think he thought about himself.

He didn't tell me about Lonnie Higgins because it was a weight on his shoulders. He told me about it for the same reason people watch the news to see if the accident they passed on the freeway gets mentioned, or the bank robbery that caused the police to block off a certain street which made them late for work. Anything can become anything to talk about if it's even remotely interesting to an outside observer.

It becomes something of a special event. There's a sort of celebrity to it. Neil Armstrong had the moon landing, and my mother bought a lottery ticket from a convenience store that sported a million dollar winner. She stood behind the counter as the local news taped a short interview with the store's clerk. Both events were featured on television. She rushed home to tune in. And for a few minutes, I think she felt truly alive. Alive in the sense that a bunch of random strangers were becoming, at least, partially aware of her existence. If they were watching that program, they wouldn't be able to miss her. Sadly, it affected me too. In a way. I looked at the television screen, at the pixilated image of my mother and thought, *how humiliating*.

Mitch had Lonnie Higgins to talk about now. And it made him feel a little bit more alive. To most people, having other people aware of them is an accomplishment all its own.

"Excuse me for a minute," I said, pushing my chair back and walking out of the office.

I made my way down the narrow hallway and stopped in the corridor right before entering the bar area. I checked to make sure Sam was doing okay. He was right where I left him. His eyes glued to the television over the bar. He was slurping something out of a dark glass with a straw. I wondered for a second if Mona would stoop to serve a prepubescent boy alcohol, but then shook that thought right out of my head. Maybe at an earlier point in her life. But not now. I caught a wave from some Mexican bastard from the small rectangular window opening into the kitchen area. There was no telling if I knew him or not. I guess I did if he recognized me, but I'll be damned if I can tell one Mexican griddle cook from another. I waved back with a smile.

"Que pas so, Frank?"

"Yep," I replied, *pshht*.

I stepped out of the corridor, just far enough to bring myself into the orbit of the neon lights decorating the walls. Beer signs. One that looked like a rooster. I skirted the wall until I came to the dart board. There was a black light above the chalkboard next to it and, casually as I could, I hovered around it, checking to see how much dried blood was on my clothes. There were countless tiny spatters. The size of pinpricks. Like stars showing through a partially cloudy night sky. *Jesus*. How had I not noticed that? A chill ran up my spine and I clenched Lonnie's panties in my fist. Disappointment kept coming at me like waves on a beach. I couldn't seem to get around it. I took the panties out of my pocket and tossed them into the nearest trash can. My original plan was to hide them in Mitch's office somewhere, just to screw with him... maybe put a little suspicion his way. But shit... if I did that now... if I got cute, I'd have to worry every day if there was some small clue I'd left behind that could put me away. And, hell... Lonnie probably would play up the rape thing. If not right after she woke up, then maybe a year afterward. Once the sympathy from her beating started to dye down. She'd have to make it worse... have some bad flashbacks... some revelations... and the sympathy would start pouring in all over again. And then she could feel special for a little while longer.

I wanted to curl up in the corner and cry. And hell, I guess I sort of did a little inside. It's always been part of my problem. A sort of continuous depression. But to be honest, I've always been more depressed just for being depressed than I was depressed for any particular reason. Just like disappointment, I can feel it coming on, and I think... *give me a break, man.* It's too much. I can't seem to get a full day of optimism going anymore. Well, not since turning thirty. I tapped the trash can with my foot, said goodbye to Lonnie's underwear, and went back to Mitch's office.

"Don't be a stranger," he said as I lifted the guitar case off his desk. He had the receiver of the office telephone cradled between his shoulder and his ear, like he was about to make a call.

"See you around," I said.

# CHAPTER 7

AS SOON AS me and the kid stepped outside, the Nevada sun came down and hit me straight in the face. I instantly felt better. Usually I didn't meet that desert heat with anything but harsh language and a squint, but as the dust clung to my shoes on the way to the car, I remembered why I'd come out here in the first place. There is something liberating about it, all of that heat and sand. If you can take the sun, if you can take the heat, it'll work with you-- it'll keep all the assholes inside, boxed in their houses, or apartments, or hotels with their air conditioners and their ice boxes, trapped; and it just leaves you with more space, a little more breathing room, a little more time to think. Just like anything else, the desert likes to be liked. I imagine if you could stare up at the sun directly, you'd see a big smiley face lookin' right back down at you. Or, at least down at me. In a way I was glad to be done with Mitch and his crappy bar. It was time to start over. Time for a fresh start. Time to flush all the baggage and hard feelings.

I dropped the guitar in its new case in the back seat of the Caddy, took a beat longer lighting my cigarette and tried not to smile too silly as I blew the smoke out. I was feeling a nice, steady rhythm and shaking my leg just a little bit, swiveled my hip a bit. Man, I really couldn't tell you why I was feeling so good. I guess the spirit was just moving me is all. Best I can explain it. I leaned over to check myself in the caddy's side mirror but Sam stood in the way.

"Watch out, Chief," I said, fluttering my fingers to brush him aside. He slid out of the way and I looked in the mirror, smoothed my hair down at the sides and popped an eyebrow. I straightened up, put my sunglasses on and looked back down at Sam. He was frowning a bit. Looking bored. Sort of lost and pathetic. To tell the truth… I sort of felt like leaving him there in the parking lot. Not like he was *my* responsibility. But, I don't know. I guess he looked up to me a little, and it's always good to have someone around who looks up to you. And, yeah… well… it was time for a fresh start.

"Why the long face?" I asked.

"I don't think that lady in there liked you very much," he said.

"Lady. What lady?"

"The lady behind the bar. I overheard her talking to one of the men at the bar and she said you were only there to beg for your job back."

"Said that, did she?"

"She said she knew when she first met you, you'd be out on the streets before long. Called you a waste of oxygen."

"Tzt…" I spat. "Shows what she knows. That lady's just a sucker, Sam. Matter of fact, they were begging me to come back. But I told them they could go to hell. That's what I said. Straight on to hell, Sam. You know what that means, right? Old enough to know what that particular phrase means?"

He nodded.

"It's an important part of growing up, knowing when to use those words. You only use those words when you know you're in the right. Know what I mean?"

He nodded again.

"Another part of growing up is knowing not to tell someone when another person is saying bad things about them. That's how people get their feeling hurt. Understand? Now, instead of telling me what some-*woman*- had to say about me… you should have just told her 'go straight to hell'. Cause you would've been in the right. And that problem would've been solved right then and there."

He looked confused, and that's exactly what I'd meant for him to be. It was the quickest way to put it out of his mind. I couldn't have him going around thinking like it mattered whether or not that old slut liked me or not. Of course, it hurt me deeply to hear she did not. It wasn't exactly a hot knife in my back… more like a sharp toothpick… just like most other things… just poking… poking. Get enough of them toothpicks and pretty soon it's like Chinese Water Torture. God damn people. Who the hell was she to criticize me? And to spew that shit in front a little kid like Sam. Fuck it all, man. What can you do? You can't be around to defend yourself at all times. Shit.

I spent a good twenty minutes in silence wondering what I could ever have done to make Mona dislike me, ever. Ever!

Fuck. It gave me the same feeling I always get

whenever I came face to face with another person's opinion of me. You try and you try…

"What are we stopping here for?" Sam asked.

"I just need to pick up something real quick," I said as I put the car in park in front of the small, used bookstore. I ran inside and let my eyes play over the signs hanging over each section till I found the small foreign language area.

My old man was in the Army, so I was a military brat. When I was about five or six the family was stationed overseas. My father went over about two months earlier than my mother and my older brother and me. Well, finally, we flew over to meet up with him. It was a seven hour flight and I was real excited to see my daddy again. When we landed we had to wait for some reason what felt like forever before we disembarked. I knew my daddy was waiting for us in the airport, and I kept saying, "I want to see my daddy. I want to see my daddy." Like I was frustrated we couldn't get off the plane. I don't remember feeling frustrated, but I must have been to be saying that over and over again. And I remember my mother shushing me, so I know I was saying it pretty loud. And the passengers nearby kept looking over. Rolling their eyes. I can't remember their faces or nothing, but I know they was hoping I would shut up. I get upset when I remember things like that. I get to feeling ashamed. And yeah, I know you can't really control yourself, or blame yourself for something you did when you were six years old, but, man… I'd just… I'd just like to not have been that kind of kid. There is nothing I can do to go back and change the discomfort I caused all those other passengers. Nothing at all. People were looking down on me already when I was just six years old. And they were probably right. I was being a nuisance. It was a fucked up part of my personality manifesting itself. It's something I will always have done. And I kind of hate myself for it. It's embarrassing.

"Hold this," I said, returning to the car and tossing the book in Sam's lap. He picked it up and flipped through it.

"You're going to learn Spanish?" he asked, looking over at me and squinting.

"Well, you know. I want to get the basics. You know."

"Uh-huh," he said.

I glared at him. "It's something I should have done a long time ago."

"Well, why didn't you?"

"Because…" I glared again. "I'm not-ah… I don't have a lot of foresight. That a good enough reason for you? You happy?"

Sam flipped through the book again, stuck his thumb in the pages and picked a word. "Cab-ay-oh. Horse," he said. He listed a few more words under his breath then looked up at me, using the book to shield his eyes from the sun. "You're going to learn how to speak to Mexicans like this?"

"What of it?"

"It'll only take you forever," he said. "You'd have to have a photographic memory to remember all these words in less than a lifetime, and then you'll have to remember which words are nouns and which are verbs, and then figure out word order if you want it to make any sense. And, they have different words for girls. You should have gotten a phrase book, instead."

I snatched the book from his hands and threw it in the back seat. "Hey, man. I already told you I just wanted the basics. You know: *hola, como-stas, adios*."

"It sounds like you already have the basics," Sam said covering the top half of his face with his hand. The sun was almost directly overhead.

I looked down at him and shook my head. "Hey... hey. You may be smarter than me, Sam. But you will never have my class," I said, feeling myself becoming annoyed. Annoyed and bitter. It was times like these I felt like swerving the car off the road into a bridge embankment. I looked to see if Sam had ever bothered fastening his seat belt. He hadn't. "Hey, click it or ticket, man. You trying to get me in trouble?" I said, reaching across him with my free hand and tugging at the safety belt. He clicked it in place and his cheeks got red.

"Sorry," he said. "I never ride in the front seat with mom. She makes me sit in the back."

"Really?" I said, genuinely curious. "Why the backseat? She don't like your breath? She think you talk too much."

He shook his head. "Nope. It's the law back home, I guess. Mom makes me sit in a special chair in the back seat."

"S-special chair in the back seat? You mean a baby

chair? Your mom got you sitting in a damn baby chair?"

He lowered his head and squinted so hard his upper lip pulled away from his front teeth. "Not a baby chair. It's a kid's chair. For, like… kids."

"You mean a toddler's chair," I laughed. "You're nine years old, Sam. That's too damn old to be strapped in a kid's chair in the back seat."

"Yeah, but I'm short. I'm too small to ride in the front seat. Mom got pulled over once and the policeman thought I was seven."

"What?" I said, not particularly to him. A part of me wanted to laugh. I mean, come on, it was kind of funny. But on the other hand… maybe it was something that weighed down heavy on him. "Well, that's alright, Sam. You got all them brains. You don't need a few extra inches."

He smiled as much as his face would let him, squinting from the sun like he was.

"And who knows. I was a late bloomer myself. Time is on your side, Sam. Pretty soon, the world will be all yours." I pulled into the parking lot of the gas station just up the street from my house, slapped him on the shoulder and smiled. And then took the Spanish dictionary to the payphone and made a… well, a stupid call.

# CHAPTER 8

RAY ONCE SAID to me that most people were like frogs stuck in a pot of water slowly being brought to a boil. It's funny how the human condition makes more sense as an animal story. It's easier that way, I think. Because people sympathize with animals. Nobody really sympathizes with other people other than in the very general sense. We can do that now. I think we ignored each other before, like when we were living in caves and shit, but somehow, somewhere along the line, they got us believing that was wrong. We've gotten lazy enough now though, and comfortable enough to ignore other human beings, for the most part. It's what comes from living in a semi civilized society. Everyone knows, for the most part, that everyone wants the same things and it's easy to assume there's enough for everyone to go around so that there's never any real problem. But... it's another thing Ray told me... once the shit falls apart... when everything goes to hell, we won't be able to ignore one another anymore. We'll just be killing each other. That's something I find sort of appealing. There's something honest about it. That's kind of how I look at people now. I try to be honest with myself. I'll meet somebody and, yeah, I may get along with them, but I'm well aware that if the circumstances are ever to change... well, I know they'd kill me quick if they could.

Maggie was up by the time Sam and I got back.

She was sitting on the couch watching television. Her legs were folded under herself, giving that nice little diamond shape to her calve muscles. At first glance I thought she wasn't wearing anything other than a shirt, but her shorts were just really, really short. Being a typical woman, she began to complain.

"Where were you?" she said. But it was obviously a question more for sport than anything else. You could tell by her demeanor she hadn't been all that worried.

"We left a note," I said, turning to Sam. "Didn't you leave a note?" Sam nodded. "He left a note."

Maggie pulled a piece of paper from under her foot, held it up. "This note says 'be back later'. I asked where you went."

I stared at Maggie, remembering what Sam had told me about her telling her sister they were staying with me. A spasm shot through my leg. "Calm down, Mags. I just took him on some errands."

"That's not the point, Frank. I was really worried."

I went to the kitchen and grabbed a soda from the fridge. "Oh, come on, Maggie. What did you think happened? You think his father snuck in and snatched him?" I stood in front of her. "He was with me. I'm not going to let anything happen to him."

She stretched out the arm holding the note. I reached out for it. Using the note as an excuse to grab her hand. I had the note with my thumb and forefinger and held onto her hand with the rest of my fingers, holding her arm up. Her shirtsleeve slid up on her shoulder and the bottom lifted up enough to see the curve of her hip. I was getting hard and swayed her arm back and forth, playing like it was a game. She smiled. I could tell she had already smoked herself out. Marijuana for breakfast, man. Whew.

"Honey, bring me a glass of water," she said to Sam.

"How long you been awake?" I asked.

"I don't know. What time is it?"

I leaned back to read the clock on the microwave, using that as an excuse to bring her hand closer to my crotch. "Almost 6:00."

"Well, then," she said, swinging her legs out and pulling her hand free. "Almost dinner time." She hopped off the couch as Sam came back with her water. "I'll make dinner tonight. What do you think, huh? I guess we should earn our keep somehow, right?"

*Fucking- A.*

"That'd be an unbelievable gesture, Mags," I said. "No shit."

She ran her hand under the kitchen faucet and glanced at me sideways. "You being sarcastic?"

"Sarcastic? Fuck no. You kidding? I hate to cook. You have no idea how often I starve myself. It's the whole time to prepare the thing- thing. I get hungry and then I see how long it takes to make something, and then I think, like I can't wait that long, and so I usually wind up not eating at all. Like a pot pie takes a whole hour to heat up. I think it's great you wanna cook. Honest."

"What would you like?" she asked, drying her hands on a dish towel.

"Huh?"

"For dinner."

"Don't know."

"I can cook almost anything.  You like pot roast?"

"Not sure."

"Well, haven't you ever had it?"

"Well, yeah.  I guess.  A long time ago.  Like when I was a kid.  And yeah… I guess I didn't mind it.  I guess.  Okay."

"Okay, what?"

"Yeah.  Pot roast would be fine."

"Good.  Cause its Sam's favorite," she said, tossing the dish towel on the counter and traipsing back down the hall toward my room.  "I just have to change and we can go to the market."

I lifted the dish towel up and returned it to its proper place, draping it over the handle to the stove. "Market?"

"The store," she called out from my room.

I kept a few paces behind her at the store, leaning against the weight of the basket, filled to overflowing with what she made crystal clear was that night's meal only.  I wondered if she was going to pay for it all.  If she was expecting me to pay for it, then of course I would have to, although it would kill a good portion of what was left of my bank account.  All for a stupid meal I could do without.  I didn't need to eat. I was sure she and Sam could do without.  To hell with her fucking '*gesture*' of politeness.  More like she just roped herself into more charity when I needed every red damn cent!  Son of a bitch!

She had trouble squeezing her change into the

pocket of her shorts, and I tried to distribute the weight of the bags as evenly as possible to keep from walking funny back to the car. Maggie hopped into the passenger seat as I loaded the bags in the back. She seemed strangely happy, I thought, for someone about to slave in the kitchen for the next couple hours. It was going to be good. I could tell already.

I didn't see the guy until I went around to the driver's side. He grabbed hold of my door just as I opened it, and I immediately noticed the missing fingers. There was no emotion on his face, but I gathered his displaying of the damaged hand was a calculated enough move. I was thankful for the extra bandaging when that hand slammed into my face, though the missing fingers made the knuckles far more effective. My head snapped back and my body managed to fall perfectly into the driver's seat, and I even sort of absent-mindedly tugged at the seat belt when my vision cleared, and I heard Maggie say something like-- "Oh, shit," or something silly like that. Very casual. As if she discovered she'd broken a nail. "Huh?" I said, swiveling my head in her direction. I felt him grab my neck and pull me back out of the car and, even through all the confusion, I was proud of myself for not flailing my arms to block any more blows to the face. I managed to stand up on my own strength and looked up at him.

"It's not you. It's not you. I'm an understanding guy," he said as he locked his hand- the good hand- around my throat. I felt my head swell with blood and thought I heard Maggie let out a scream, but I couldn't be too sure.

I started thinking about things like cartoon rabbits and Claymation figurines, the kind I made as a kid, or wanted to-- and tin foil in the microwave and things like that. I felt the asphalt against my face and heard a few foggy epithets, and that's how I figured out he'd let me go and turned his attention to Maggie. I coughed and rubbed my throat and rose up on my hands and knees. I saw him pulling Maggie from the passenger seat, and her making it as difficult as possible for him. She dropped to the ground, lying flat like a passive activist in protest, crying and babbling, and he screamed at her about his son, and kidnap, and... um. I just sat there on my knees, feeling my saliva catch in my throat as I swallowed, and watched. Suddenly it became very interesting. I watched it as if it were something on television. Just observing. And I found myself in complete and total admiration for the mother fucker! This guy was a man. He poked and jabbed and hovered over Maggie like it was... like it was something out of Animal Kingdom; and the missing fingers just made him seem all the more dominant an animal... like a Marine Corps. General missing an eye, barking out orders wearing an eye patch, almost like he could see better because of it.

I was still a little bleary. A part of me wanted to help Maggie out, but man... I couldn't very well reason with the guy, could I? I mean, she did cut half his hand off and run away with his only son. Wasn't he entirely justified? I climbed into the car, positioning myself in the driver's seat, and checked my face in the rear view mirror. There was a welt on my forehead. I licked my finger and rubbed the welt, then turned to see as Maggie was put in a sort of Judo hold, with her arm bent behind her back. She was screaming and it amazed me how no passersby had gotten involved. No police. No nothing. I put the key in the ignition, hit the gas pedal a couple times then turned the key. The engine hesitated and I could smell fumes. I'd flooded the engine. I waited a few seconds. Wiped the sweat from my forehead, brushed the hair out of my face and looked back to see Maggie trying to crawl away from her husband. He had hold of the waist of her pants and followed behind her as if she were a dog on a leash. I let out a sort of moan and turned the key again. The engine turned, then caught. I put it in gear and drove off so fast the tires squealed. I hoped Maggie hadn't heard that.

I don't remember taking a full breath the whole way home. Just short, little panicky breaths until I got inside and splashed water over my face. I leaned in real close to the bathroom mirror and studied the welt right under my hairline. There was a scrape on my cheek that was already scabbing over. It wouldn't leave a mark, but it would look like bad acne for a couple of days. I lifted my jaw and tensed up the skin of my neck but there wasn't any bruises... at least not yet. It did hurt to swallow though.

I tuned off the water, rapped my knuckles on the edge of the sink and shuffled about in front of the mirror for a few seconds, then walked out to the living room and picked up the phone. I rapped it against the palm of my hand, trying to calm my breathing before dialing the number I usually dial when I'm worked up. I swallowed hard as it rang on the other end, but it didn't seem like anybody was going to answer. I grunted loudly and threw the phone at the couch. I slumped down beside where it landed and rubbed the little welt rising up on my forehead. That's when I heard the E chord being strummed out on my back porch. A chill went down my spine and I got up to peer out my back window. There was a man with his back to me, sitting on a folding chair and strumming away on one of my guitars. I recognized the tune. Love me Tender. He played it slowly. As if he were out of practice, just feeling it out. I slid open the screen door and stood and stared out at him.

"Es Bonita no casa?" the man said in an airy voice, slightly over pitched.

"Huh?" I said.

The man chuckled. "Yeah, hell. My Spanish isn't so good either. You'd think it would be, my line of work. But I never did take to it." He spoke casually, not turning to face me. He plucked through the strings one more time then flipped the guitar around before standing it gently against the house. "A little out of tune," he said.

"Something I can help you with?" I asked.


Okay…I guess I can go ahead and get this off my chest.

Lonnie Higgins lived in one of those shit bag, no lease month to month apartment complexes that everybody seems to land in when they first get into town. For the most part, people either set themselves into better digs after a few months, after they've gotten a little bit of cash saved up, or they high tail it out of the city and go back home. Back to mom and dad. Or back to the wife and kids. But there are always a few deadbeat, meth addicted, alcoholic pieces of shit that stick around for years and years and years, skating by just enough to get that rent by the end of the month; their presence is enough to turn these places into the shit bags that they are and, more often than not, they live in the corner apartment on the bottom floor. If it weren't for those sons of bitches, the property managers would up the rent and start calling the units condos. So I guess a piece of shit is always good for something. I was thinking about that as I sat in my car, parked on the opposite side of the street from Lonnie's complex, waiting for the filthy piece of shit in the corner apartment, the one directly under hers, to go inside. It was nearly one in the morning. The piece of shit… I call him a piece of shit, mostly it's a generalization. Kinda like calling a black man a thief. Anyhow, the piece of shit might be a nice guy, albeit a drug addicted, alcoholic- -and I could see the black filth under his toenails all the way from where I was at, and just from the light coming from a cracked yellow street lamp; but he might have been a nice guy all the same. Maybe. I don't know.

He was smoking a cigarette and fanning himself. The lumpy flesh under his arm bouncing in the air and rebounding with each wave. His slapped his hand over his pale, fleshy legs, sticking out of his shorts, like diseased elephant trunks as he blubbered something or other, loud and obnoxiously, in a deep discussion with himself. And yes, the nasty toenails. It was all very disgusting and far, far from unusual. The man's hair was a filthy grey but I would have laid odds that he was just in his early forties. I found it ironic that the man felt the need to smoke his cigarette outside. He certainly didn't seem the type to keep his apartment fresh and clean. The piece of shit.

Finally, he went inside, slamming the door loudly. And I got out of my car and walked quickly across the street, looking in every direction to make sure I wasn't seen. I didn't have any clear idea in my mind what exactly I was doing there, I think, even up to the time I got to her door. I think, in the forefront of my mind, I had the idea of maybe just joshing her a bit... teasing her maybe for running around with Mitch, who was old enough to be her father. I think... well, I think I knew that was bullshit even as I was thinking it.

I stood in front of her door. It was dark and in the shadows. The complex was much too cheap to think about things like the safety and security of its tenants. I flipped my cell phone open and scrolled through the calls until I found Lonnie's number from when Mitch had called me from her phone. I pushed send and pressed my ear to her door. A cheesy jingle played on the other side of the door... some tune from a television show. I couldn't place it. It stopped and I heard Lonnie answer her phone. There was a slight hesitation from her '*Hello*' on the other side of the door and the '*Hello*' over the phone. I hung up and redialed. What show was her ring tone from? I almost had it when she answered again. And again I hung up.

It was a cop show. No. No. No. One of those lawyer shows. Shit.

I dialed again.

This time, there was a sharpness in her voice. An impatience. "Hello," she said.

"Come to your door," I said.

When I heard the deadbolt flip, I pulled my t-shirt up over my face, resting the collar on the bridge of my nose. To Lonnie's credit, when she opened the door and saw me, she didn't hesitate to slam the door back shut. Unfortunately for her, I had time to jam my foot in the crack. I pushed the door open and went inside. It was very bright in her apartment. Every single light was on. I looked around quickly to make sure she was alone and saw the beer cans strewn all over the place, the dirty dishes piling up in the sink, a few dead cockroaches on the floor under her table. Lonnie had backed herself against a wall and stared at me with her eyes all big. Her bottom lip quivered and she breathed uneasy. I looked up from the floor and at her, then craned to look in her bedroom, where I saw her bed was covered with pillows and stuffed animals, dozens of them, as if she thought she could be a princess in at least one part of her world. Some kind of sweet girl. It boggled my mind that a girl could have a bed like that but be such a shit-ass. But I guess most women are like that, right?

I walked up real close to her and just stared at her. I

was beginning to breath hard, myself, and was beginning to feel kinda nauseous. I held my hand up and was almost going to tell her to give me a minute. To let me collect myself. But instead I slapped her on the side of the face.

She slapped me back. Neither of us slapped the other very hard. In her case, I gather, it was instinctual. Like maybe she had a couple brothers that used to pick on her when she was growing up. But that was good. That was good. It taught her a little how to take care of herself.

Her hand had pushed my t-shirt down a little, but not enough to uncover my face. I pulled it back up where it was, and punched her closed fisted on the side of her face. She bounced back against the wall and shifted a bit to the side, but she didn't run or fall to the floor or nothing. But it hadn't been a hard punch either. I still felt sick. There had been an impotence in my swing. It felt kind of like throwing a punch in a dream. You know how that feels... when your body isn't moving because you're asleep... but your brain keeps trying to put some force into the punch. It was exactly like that. I opened and shut my fingers to pump more blood through my veins, then punched her again. This time hard. Right smack in the middle of her face. There was a sickening crack and she shifted again. She covered her face with her hand and stared at me with bunny rabbit eyes. A tear rolled down one cheek and her face was already starting to swell. Then she began to scream. I wrapped my hand around her face and slammed the back of her head into the wall a couple of times. The first push was nice and strong but the following two or three were really just me going through the motions. It was more like I was making her nod yes to an unasked question. But there was still a good sized hole in the sheet rock, and a small blot of blood mixed in with some hair.

I let her fall to the floor and turned my back on her. I pulled the shirt down off my face and took a series of quick, deep breaths. I was getting dizzy and had to prop myself up with my hands on my thighs. I dry heaved a couple of times. It was a little embarrassing, and I inched a little bit into the kitchen so she wouldn't see me having a spell. I turned the faucet on her kitchen sink and scooped a couple handfuls of cool water into my mouth, then rubbed my face with my wet hand. The pile of dirty dishes in the sink were crusted over with old food-stuffs and mold. There was a tea cup filled halfway with cigarette ash, and a saucer with about a dozen cigarette butts. A tiny spider floated in the greasy water of a soaking pot. God damn, it was revolting.

I went back to where Lonnie was curling slowly into a ball as if her muscles were constricting. Like a snake that's had its head cut off. I nudged her with my foot, then kicked her between her shoulder blades. "Hey. Hey. Look," I said, bending down over her. She turned her head just-a-little-bit, and she let out a long, lilting moan that almost seemed to be pushed out of her. It sounded as if her soul floated on the air coming out of her lungs… like- like it was the exact kind of noise she was supposed to make. "Oh, man," I said, straightening up and tucking my fingers into my pants back pockets. It was captivating, that sound. It was just right. I realized I was wearing a silly grin. "Hey. Okay." I bent down over her again. "It's alright," I said, shaking her shoulder. I grabbed her wrist, lifted her arm and let it drop. When I was a kid, I saw a show about monkeys and that's what they always did to see if a hurt monkey was still alive. They sort of toss its arm up and let it drop. I mean... it's what they do in professional wrestling too. Like if one wrestler has the other in some really badass hold, like the Figure Four Leg Lock, or the Camel Clutch... and the other wrestler passes out from the pain, the ref does that monkey trick with the arm, and if it drops three times, the ref calls the match quits. It's almost fucking universal.

All of a sudden, she began flopping around. I balanced myself on my heels and leaned back. Then, just as suddenly, she was still again. Here head started rolling and her mouth opened wide and she started making a '*Whup-whup*' sound. Like she wasn't getting any air. I almost started laughing but, actually, I was beginning to feel a little bad. Her eyes were all swollen and her mouth was opening wide and puckering, making ugly ass pucker shapes like a fish out of water. I put my hand on her forehead and leaned in. I crawled over on top of her and clamped my knees down over her arms and ripped her shirt down from the collar.

She was breathing a little better with her head pushed back, but she was clearly struggling. I leaned in slowly and put my mouth over hers and blew some air into her lungs. I raised up, licked my lips, and then gave her a couple more breaths until she didn't seem to have no more problem breathing on her own. And then suddenly I was wondering what the hell the point of my being there was.

And then I started to get mad that I was there at all. And I started to get mad at Lonnie for letting me do what I was doing to her. And for making me feel bad. Making me feel a little depressed.

I punched her again, ramming my fist into her naked torso. A rib cracked and I punched her a couple more times. Her bra popped open and her breasts flopped out, bouncing side to side as I hit her. I grabbed her left titty and twisted it pretty hard. She screamed then. I took my hand off her forehead and pressed my palm under her chin and clamped her mouth shut. She kept trying to scream but it only came out in muffled grunts, animal like groans. Just like a woman. I shifted my weight further up on her stomach, setting all my weight down on her abdomen, and slapped her breasts with both sides of my other hand. I noticed her nipples tightening up and I stopped, straightened up and placed my hands on my waist. Now, I just want to put it out that I wasn't being perverted or nothing batting her titties around like that. There wasn't anything sexual about it. And I didn't get no kind of arousal or anything... that's seedy. Uh, but... yeah. I'm no rapist or anything like that. I don't think I could do that. I just don't think I have it in me. So forget all that shit Mitch said.

Lonnie quieted down, then. Except for a very low, kind of pulsing hiccup every few seconds, she seemed as peaceful as a dove. I took a big gulp of fresh air and looked down at her. I stared down at her and tried to remember what she looked like the first time I saw her. She had been sitting at one of the tables at Mitch's Place, filling out an application. But I could tell by the wink Mitch gave me and the silly, childish lift of his eyebrows that the application was hardly necessary. She was far too attractive and young for that kind of formality. The only use Mitch had with her application was to figure out how persuasive he would have to be with her later. I remember walking past her with my gear. My guitar and my amp. And feeling a little funny. A little queasy. And a little uneasy. I wondered if she was still going to be there at that table when I started playing. I wondered what she would think of me after seeing that. And I wondered if there were any way she could think that before seeing it. Her eyes were bright green.

I couldn't see her eyes now. Not very well anyhow. Her left eye was closed up tight and swollen about the size of a golf ball. Her right eye was bruised black, but it was open just a slit. I couldn't see the green of her pupils very well through the glassiness. I tried to stare into that eye… and then her head started to roll again. Slowly. Slowly. I pulled my t-shirt back over my face as her face turned up and she tried to look at me through that little slit of bruised up flesh. And then I saw just a teeny, tiny bit of that green. Damn. Poor girl.

"I'm particularly partial to this drain you got dug in the dirt here next to your porch," the guy said, ignoring my question, as if we were just continuing on with a conversation we'd been having already. "I imagine that prevents flooding during the monsoon season, am I right? Yeah, I had to do something similar in my back yard a couple years back. It's a lot of work, but a heckuva good investment. Did you dig that yourself, Frank?" Do you mind if I call you Frank?"

My first instinct was to answer his question… both of them, but I just stared at him for a few seconds before going back inside to get my .38.

But as I shuffled through the drawer I couldn't find it. Had I left it in the glove compartment? Dang it, man.

"Don't bother, Frank," the man said, walking up behind me. "I already pocketed that pea shooter. You wouldn't want to go waving that thing at me anyhow, buddy, let me tell ya."

He laughed, and I felt my body tense. Nausea spread over me, making me sweat. My heart was racing like a million miles an hour. I felt like I couldn't move a muscle if I had to. And I began imaginin' all the fucked up stuff this guy could do to me if he really wanted to. And I was thinking, it's like this, isn't it? This is the kind of guy I am?

"Now what would you go and do a thing like that for?" I asked, turning to him with a smile. "It's not your property is it?"

The guy smiled back, and it was like he was chewing on some bubble gum, the way the little muscles in his jaw were working. His eyes like… bugged out at me, all piercing blue, but I couldn't keep my eyes off his hair, man. He had a cowboy hat on, but there was a little wisp of wheat blonde hair sort of brushing over his eyes. And his face was real round, so he looked sort of childish. He kinda looked like a football coach from the early eighties. But even then, I sure didn't want to push him. Guy just waltzes into your house like that… he's gotta be sure about something, right?

He stared at me for a while, being real quiet… and I could tell he was trying to get me to look him in the eye. But I couldn't. Man, I just can't do that kind of thing. And after he gave up on that, he pointed his finger at me, like it was the barrel of a gun, and his thumb was the hammer, and he smiled.

"You ain't even worried about the kid, are ya? You didn't even notice he wasn't here." He laughed real loud, like a balloon popping. "You're something else, partner. You really are."

All his talking had calmed me down. I don't know, there was something soothing about the way he spoke. Kind of easy going. I relaxed a little and leaned against the dresser.

"What were you thinking, Frank?" he asked me then, his face getting a little serious. "How much did you think you were going to get?"

I thought about answering that, too, just… just cause, but he kept on talking.

"And man, your Spanish," another laugh. "Your Spanish is worse than mine. We had to… ha! We had to listen to the message about *fifteen* times just to make out what… what we thought you were trying to say."

Tears were coming to his eyes, he was trying to

hold back the laughter so hard. He even braced himself against me for a brief second until he could go on. "Yeah, lucky for us we were already in town. We got here… shit, about a week ago after we got your first call. Just figured Vegas was the closest town some shit like this might happen… and I guess we were right. Right, Frank? Didn't take much to find out who Maggie was acquainted with out here. And that's you. And so we ran a quick trace on that last call, and god damn if it wasn't giving us a bead right around your house."

"Hey man, I didn't… I didn't ask her to come here."

"I know that, Frank. I know that. Stupid bitch was just runnin' scared is all. There ain't nothing much more to it. I'm surprised you let her stay, to tell the truth. But I guess, the ol' girl still has her looks, so you were probably fishing to fuck her, am I right? Hell, I'd fuck her, Frank. If I weren't working for her husband, that is. But the fact of the matter is I'd probably still do it."

I nodded.

"Did you fuck her, Frank?" he asked, smiling real big. I mean real big. It was creepy.

And I imagined fucking Maggie, or really, just imagined Maggie naked and flopping around like she was getting fucked, but I didn't see myself in there, or anybody. It was like she was getting fucked by the invisible man or something. And I guess, I guess the s-situation kind of made it difficult for me to see myself in that position.

"Did you fuck her, Frank?"

"Why, hell no, I didn't fuck her," I spat. "God damn, man. Ain't that kind of thing private, anyhow?"

That's when he pulled my .38 from his front pocket. At least, I'm pretty sure it was mine.

"There ain't nothing private about infidelity," he said, and pointed that thing right at my melon.

I can't be sure now if I didn't piss myself none. But I'm almost certain it didn't happen. I did say, "Oh, god, Jesus," though, out loud. Like I couldn't help it at all. It just blurted out on its own, man. And I felt like one of those little girls that would cry when the King would walk out on stage. They couldn't help themselves neither.

I felt the muzzle of the .38 press right up on my temple. I could hear the whiskers of my sideburn brush up against the metal. And that was my head, man. I ain't never been more aware of my own head before in all my life. It's like that was all I was at that moment. Like a damn... like a damn piñata head, taking up the whole room, just waiting to be busted open. And all my thoughts were just... just candy.

I was really in a bind, man. Heck, going all the way back to fourth grade, a guy didn't deny makin' it with a chick. Ever. Even if he never ever saw her before, or heard of her. It's just not the way we work, even if we weren't exactly sure what 'making' it meant. So I really had to think hard about what I was supposed to say to this guy. I was pretty sure my answer was a factor in whether or not he pulled the trigger. I figure I was supposed to say "no", which was more or less the truth… but shit, man… it's funny… I kinda thought about saying "yes".

And then I did start to wonder what happened to Sam. Did this guy pick him up around the same time he stole my gun? Was the boy stuffed in the backseat of his car, or in the trunk? Or was Sam hiding out somewhere in the house, like under the bathroom counter or something? I thought about my brains being blown out, and Sam walking in to see me like that, with my brains splattered all over the wall like a mess of spaghetti. And then I started thinking about all the other awkward shit that goes along with being dead. Like how, if the guy did shoot me, what sort of position would I land in, and would it look strange or effeminate. If he shot me in the face, would it blow some of my teeth out, and then I'd have a, like a fuckin' toothless corpse. Not to mention how you supposedly shit yourself. And then there's the autopsy and some weird guy cutting your heart open and playin' with your penis and stuff, and writing it all down so there's nothing left of you. That's it. End of story. Finito.

"So where is the kid, anyway?" I asked, trying to sound like all this was a joke I was in on.

He leaned back a bit, tried lookin' in my eyes again and pursed his lips out, like he was trying to work something out of his teeth with his tongue. "Oh, he's alright. By now he's back with his daddy. Not that it's any of your damn business, though, right? But then again, I guess maybe it is sort of your business. I mean, you were hoping to get some cash for him, right? Which brings us back to that question of how much you were asking. So how much, Frank? Thirty thousand? Forty thousand? How much is it worth to you? And let's see, should we subtract what you musta paid to fuck that whore of a mother of his?"

I crooked my head a bit, just to get the tip of the .38 off my scalp. "Hey, man. That's not very nice. I never said I fucked her."

I saw his Adam's apple bob as he swallowed hard, and his mouth turned up in a sneer. "Jesus Christ," he said, and tossed a handkerchief at me. "I ain't even hit you yet and you're already bleeding."

I caught the handkerchief and turned to look at myself in the mirror above my dresser. Sure enough, my nose had begun to bleed again.

"Ugh. That's twice," I said, sort of nasally as I pinched my nostrils shut.

"You're some kind of pepper, Frank," he said. And laughed. "Let's just take it easy on you then."

I wanted to tell him not to laugh at me. That it… but then he hit me upside my head, I think with the handle of the .38. A bright light flashed behind my eyes and then darkness. And that was that for a while.

# CHAPTER 9

WHEN I WOKE up, the blood from my nosebleed had dried and mixed with the blood from the gash over my eye. I lifted my head and heard a sort of subdued Velcro like sound as the dried blood peeled away from the carpet. I stood up and looked in the mirror. It took me a few seconds to recognize myself. I looked like some sort of god damn Indian savage. Small tufts of carpet fuzz was stuck in the crusted blood and I sort of laughed a little. I clicked on the table lamp on the dresser and leaned in closer to the mirror to pick out the fuzz. It was a painstaking effort, man. Some of the fuzz had dried where the blood coagulated up in my eyelashes and eyelids. And it required a certain amount of dexterity to keep it from stinging too bad.

I stumbled out to the kitchen and grabbed a beer from the fridge, then sat down at the kitchen table and chugged it down. I stared across to the stove and sniffed and thought about how I was supposed to be having a pot roast that night. I had actually been looking forward to it. A real meal, cooked by a woman, and with a kid in the mix, it woulda been like... kinda like a family dinner.

The blood around my mouth smeared across the opening of the beer bottle, and that tangy, metallic, taste mixed with the beer, which didn't make all that big a difference, but still, I guessed I'd better wash my face.

I went to the bathroom, took a leak and scrubbed the blood from my face, then sat down to ponder the events of the evening.

Poor Maggie. I wondered what she was going through at that particular moment. What does a man do to a woman after she's cut his hand off and led him on some kinda crazy wild goose chase? I mean, this wasn't some argument over finances, or dry cleaning. This was some serious stuff. I imagine he'd have to take it out on her in some way or other. Probably sexual. I mean, they'd been married for a few years, and she'd had a kid and all, so I'm sure he was a little bored with her even before all that shit started. But now... man I bet there was a lot of excitement. A lot of excitement, and... pent up frustration. And then I imagined Maggie like I did before, naked and moaning and squirming around like some invisible man was really giving it to her good. And I sat down on the toilet and masturbated about it for a while. Like an hour. But I just couldn't make anything happen. Couldn't finish. I wasn't feeling too good.

"Well, shit," I said. Then got up and put some gauze over the cut above my eye.

On my way from the bathroom I kicked something with my foot. Whatever it was went sliding across the floor to hit the wall on the other side of the living room. I knelt down and saw my .38 next to the floor vent. The son of a bitch had dropped it after he hit me with it. I smiled as I bent to pick it up, caressed it a little and looked real close to see if any of my blood had stained in the diamond shaped grooves of the wooden grip. Nope. Clean as a whistle. Unloaded too.

How do you like that? Now I felt like an even bigger sucker than I did before.

I stuffed the gun into my back pocket and paced around my living room for a while, trying to wrap my head around something meaningful… something comfortable and familiar. I felt like my head had to be put back together, man, like Maggie and Sam and Lonnie and Mitch and all the other fuckers had just made a mess of my spirit. I couldn't feel that ol' comfy feeling I knew as me. It was all other people. And other people's shit, man. It was just bringing me down. It was hard not to get pissed about it, no matter how hard I tried not to.

I could feel a headache coming on and pressed my thumbs into my temples, but that just made it hurt worse 'cause of all the beatings I'd been taking. I chewed half a bottle of aspirin and slumped down by the window. Stared out at my front porch, pictured the football coach from the eighties just standing there, full of surly confidence. Like he already knew he could show up and start pushin' me around, threaten me. And he hadn't even met me. Hadn't ever seen me before in his whole life. He just knew. I don't know, man. Does that say more about him or me?

That surly confidence was Elvis Pressley's whole shtick, man. And I always thought I had a little of that... but I guess I didn't really have it. Not like I thought I did.

The mother fucking football coach from the eighties had it. But not me. It made my stomach turn to think about it. But who knows, man... maybe there's only a certain amount of that shit to go around in this world, and maybe it's like... what do you call it... precipitation, and maybe some people got it a little more some days and a little less on others. Maybe that's it. And so maybe this just wasn't one of my days, man.

I shook my head. Oh, man. I had to get out of there. Out of that house. All I could think of was that man stepping through my front door- walking down my hallway, as if he'd had all the permission in the world. And it was just like me to start hating this little piece of my life because some asshole had decided to pollute it. I wouldn't ever be able to stand in my own bedroom again without remembering that shit. It was already working its way into my brain like a... like a damn boll weevil.

I raced outside and hopped into the caddy. And before I knew it I was hauling ass down the county road heading south away from town.

Whether my nose started bleeding again, or I didn't fix up the wound the coach had given me, it's hard to say. But after a while I began to notice my face feelin' wet, and I could taste it a little around the corners of my mouth. I shouted a couple curses and tried like hell to ignore it, to put it on the back burner. But it started caking up and makin' my face feel like I was wearin' one of those, like clay masks women use to clear their pores of blackheads. And I checked myself in the rearview mirror, wiped my face with my sleeve, wondering if I could peel the layer of blood away in one big piece just exactly like those masks… and meanwhile I'm barreling down the road at 60 miles per hour.

I felt the front end buckle a bit, and then the car started vibrating like as if I had a giant boom box in the trunk, and next thing I know the caddy's flying off the road. I just barely saw the coyote flip up and crack the windshield before I slammed on the brakes and skid to a stop about ten yards into the brush. My head had pressed against the steering wheel so hard, man, you'd think it was part of me. But that wasn't so bad. I was pretty numb up there already.

I blinked, took a look around. I might as well have been on Mars. I noticed blood dripping down on my shirt and started to wipe it away, but when I tried to move my arm, a sharp pain blasted my entire right side. When my vision cleared I had a look at my arm, and I ain't no doctor or anything, but it looked pretty broke to me. My elbow was all puffed up and purple, and my forearm was hanging limply loose.

"Aw, man," I sort of moaned.

*This is some bullshit.*

I unclicked my safety belt… yeah, I guess it worked, and stepped out of the caddy. I slipped a little in the loose sand the tire had gouged out and hurt my arm again as I caught myself from taking a header in the dirt. I winced, doubled over a bit and hugged my bad arm with the good one, took a few deep breaths, and then stepped back to view the damage.

The caddy didn't look all that bad. A few dings here and there as far as I could tell. Both tires on the left side were blown to hell though so I wasn't getting out of there anytime soon. I shook my head again, got dizzy and fell. Nearly broke my ass on a sharp rock, but missed it and laughed for some reason I'm still not sure about. Then I managed to pull myself back to my feet and have a look around. I could see the road stretching away for miles, but there weren't no one else about. It was creepy, man. Just miles and miles of nothing. I wondered how it must have felt for the first white men to make it out here... having to worry about Indians crawling out from under rocks and poking from behind cactus, shooting arrows from every direction... taking scalps and all that mess. And the blood pouring down my face just made me feel like that had already happened to me. Maybe my whole life had been some weird fever dream that started as soon as ol' Geronimo's blade started sawing into me.

Then I remembered seeing that coyote bounce off the windshield and started looking around for it. I found it about a hundred yards down the road. I stood over the mangy creature, looking down at it for a while. It wasn't moving... well, almost. Its chest was pounding 'cause it was breathing so hard, but other than that it lay still. Its eyes were wide and just staring straight ahead like it didn't see me any.

"You okay, boy?" I asked it, with a flutter in my voice.

I could see blood staining a small patch of its fur behind its shoulder blades, but other than that it didn't look all that bad. But the way it was just lying there, the way it was breathing so rapidly, making little screechy noises as it exhaled, had me believing it was pretty beat up inside. Well, I supposed there was nothing for it. Best to put it out of its misery.

I limped to pick up a rock and lifted it with my good arm. I raised it up and took aim at the poor thing's head. Hoping to crush the skull and end it quick. Mercy killin', right? Ain't that what they call it?

The fucking thing just kept staring straight ahead. Didn't even look up at me, like it was... like it just couldn't face it, maybe. And then I started crying. And I dropped the rock and sat down on the road next to it. I stroked the fur of its stretched out neck and cried some more, feeling the guilt fill my guts like a damn black cancer. If I hadn't decided to take a joy ride, this little creature would be running free, having the time of its life... feeling the wind in its face... shit, man. How could I do something like this?

A long time ago, around the time I got my driver's license, I ran over the carcass of an already dead dog, and it took me almost a whole week to get that out of my mind. Believe it or not, I felt that way about all kindsa road kill. Dogs, cats, armadillos, squirrels... squirrels affect me the most, 'cause I just, I just like squirrels a whole lot... you ever watch those things jumping around, like tiny furry acrobats... and I always say a little prayer when I see 'em on the side of the road 'cause it's like… a desecration almost to see them like that.

I kept on crying and wheezing and making the same sounds the coyote made as it breathed. And then I lay down next to it, resting my head on its ribs… feeling my head lift and fall with its breathing… and it felt… it just felt real nice. And I felt myself losing consciousness… felt myself lifting away a little.

I could barely make out all the sounds and movement and flashing lights. And it just felt like I was going someplace better, man. Someplace where none of my life ever happened, and never could. The only thing I was absolutely certain about was the coyote. Just me and the coyote. And I didn't fight it at all. I mean that, man.

# CHAPTER 10

IT FELT LIKE a colony of ants was marching up my wrist, circling in the palm of my hand, and my imagination went ahead and ran with it, until I could see, like, a dark, swirling galaxy in the palm of my hand, leeching out to the crease lines in my skin, the life line.

"Hey, hey- keep your hands off me, you damn, jive-ass degenerate," I shouted before realizing it was a doctor checking up on me. He'd been brushing my palm with his fingers.

I'd wound up in the hospital, of course, completely missing the entire ambulance ride. I have no memory of it showing up, or when it did. I have no idea who called for it. Who could have seen me so far outside of town? I guess it was Indians, man. Only explanation. And hell, I guess they're not all bad. Let that be your proof.

My broken arm was wrapped in a cast from my wrist up past my elbow, and it was already itching like crazy. I'd been in an out of consciousness while they were setting the arm and stitching me up, and I guess I needed a transfusion, so I don't remember hardly anything before coming to with the doc fiddling with my hand. I'd sat up so fast, all the blood rushed from my head and I had to lay back down to keep the room from spinning.

"Just take it easy, Frank," said the doc, scratching something on a chart next to the bed.

"Did the ky-ote make it?" I asked, softly.

"The ky-ote?" the doc replied.

"Yeah, man. I hit it with my car. It musta still been there when you all found me. It was stickin' by my side. I don't think it was goin' anywhere."

"Ah, yes. The coyote. Yes. Yes, well, don't worry about that, Frank. Animal control took it in. It's going to be just fine."

I smiled and felt myself drifting back to sleep. "That's good, man. That's good. Thank you, doc," I mumbled, and that was it for a while.

When I woke up again a nurse or nurse's aide or whatever they're called was opening up the window blinds, letting the sunlight flood the room. I was reminded of the cast when I tried to cover my eyes and almost broke my own nose.

"Hey, hey," I called out to the lady before she could leave the room. She stopped and smiled. "Hey, how long do I gotta be in here?" I asked. But I guess she didn't feel like answering me 'cause she just waltzed right out of the room without paying me no more mind. Fucking cunt. Probably didn't speak English. The whole place is getting overrun by foreigners.

I flicked the cast with my finger, trying to get at an itch and stared out the window. There wasn't much of a view, but I could see the tops of some buildings, mostly the other wings of the hospital. I don't mind that kind of view so much, mostly because I like birds, and there's always birds pecking around rooftops. And I'm not just talking about pigeons either. I've seen all kinds of birds hanging round parking garages and shit. Blue jays, cardinals, blackbirds, of course, and a whole heck of a lot of grackles. It's funny to see them all fluttering around each other but not really having much to do with one another. Birds of a feather and all that. It's kinda comforting knowing all those birds aren't just up there doing it with each other. That's just chaos, man.

Chaos in the skies. It's a good name for a song.

So I watched the birds and thought about birds... and all the thinking about birds got me to thinking about the coyote I'd hit. I knew the doc was lying. There's no way the poor mutt could have survived. Animal control wouldn't waste any resources on something like that. Damn paramedics probably just ignored it while they were taking care of me. And then I started thinking about the coyote laying there by itself, panting and bleeding, all alone, watching the ambulance take me away... not moving its head or blinking its eyes... just watching the road, maybe twitching its whiskers... and me going away in the ambulance... and the sky getting darker and darker and it getting colder and colder.

I scraped my cheek with the cast trying to wipe away the tears. It just felt bad, man. Just a real heavy feeling. Yet another thing I couldn't undo.

And then I started thinking about the football coach...man, I wish I'd gotten a name from the bastard. Probably something like, Charles, or Bruce, or Steel. You had to wonder where a guy like that comes from. A factory made hard-ass. Or maybe I'm just talking him up because he embarrassed me. Who knows with things like that? Of course, I guess it ain't too hard to embarrass me either.

As I was watching the birds, I heard a rustle at the edge of my bed and saw a Mexican cleaning out the trash can. Well, maybe he was Guatemalan or El Salvadoran or something. I don't mean nothin' by it but they all look and smell the same.

"Hey man, is it okay if I just get on out of here?" I asked him, sort of quiet so as not to disturb or spook him.

He emptied the room's small trash can into a large trash bag and stared at me... for what felt like a real long time. Now I was getting spooked.

"You speak English, chief?"

The Mexican's eyes got wide, practically popping out of his head, and he said... "Elvis... Elvis Pressley?"

And that brought a big 'ol smile to my face. "Yeah... yeah I knew you spoke a little English," I said and slapped him on the shoulder.

"Elvis Pressley," he said again and then a bunch of other shit I couldn't understand. But I smiled and nodded anyway just to be polite.

"Yeah, man... so I'm just gonna scoot on out of here," I told him. "Before they start asking about insurance. And I know you understand about that." And I laughed out loud which got him laughing too. He was still laughing when I walked out of the room. Who knows, man? Maybe what I said in English was something real funny in Spanish.

It must've been a quiet night because I didn't see anyone in the hallway. There weren't none of those noises and running around you see in the movies. Matter of fact, it was so quiet, I had to pick up my feet to try and keep my footsteps from bouncing off the walls, sounding like a damn snare drum. I saw the front desk up ahead like it was the light at the end of the tunnel. And then I started wondering where the hell I was going to. I didn't really want to go home. And it wasn't just because of the coach, either. To tell the truth, believe it or not, I was kinda upset about Maggie not being there anymore. And I guess Sam, too. And then I started getting upset about that, and my throat got all quivery. And yeah, I guess I was lonely. The end of the corridor opened into the waiting room which was carpeted, so my footsteps weren't causing me so much anxiety by the time I reached the front desk.

"Can you tell me which room Lonnie Higgins is in?" I asked the lady at the counter.

I gave a light knock on the door to her room, even though the stopper was keeping it propped wide open. I wasn't sure if she was awake or not. The overhead lights were off so the only light came from the small lamp on the cabinet next to her bed. I poked my head into the room and took a look at her. She was lying partially on one side, facing away from the door and toward the window even though the blinds were drawn, and I could see that her eyes were open. I cleared my throat, guessing she hadn't heard my knocking, and tapped on the door again. You have to announce yourself. You can't just walk into someone's room uninvited. She turned her head slowly and looked at me.

"Hey," I said quietly. "You recognize me?"

She didn't say anything for a few seconds. It felt like forever. And I could see her mind working behind the eye that wasn't swollen practically shut. Both of them were bruised up pretty badly, like she was wearing too much mascara and, don't get me wrong, but it made her look a whole lot prettier than I remembered. Finally she smiled… or I guess did the best she could, like she was too damn weak to exert herself even that much.

"Hi, Frank," she said.

I took that as an invitation and walked over to sit in the chair by her bedside. The lamp was positioned so that the light fell on the both of us, enveloping us in a soft, yellowish glow.

"I guess they got you on some pretty serious painkillers, huh?" I said, not really knowing what to say.

She didn't respond to that, but I took that to mean she was too beat to waste the energy on the obvious. I looked around, staring at all the flowers and cards her well-wishers had brought. It was more than I expected for a girl who didn't have any family near about, or many friends to speak of. Unless I just didn't know her as well as I thought I had. Heck, maybe she had lots of friends. She was pretty enough. Good looking people don't seem to have much trouble making friends. Good looking women at least.

"What happened to you?" she asked me. Her voice sounded fragile, like she was sleepy, or just waking up. Her eyes were on my cast.

"Oh," I mumbled, shrugging the cast. "Hit and run. If you can believe it."

"Oh-no," she said.

"Yep. It was my own fault though. I wasn't at a crosswalk or nothing. But, I guess it's not so bad. The car was moving pretty fast. I'm lucky all I got was this busted wing."

I smiled.

"I've always hated the way people drive here," she said, staring up at the ceiling. Her eyes were glassed over. The prettiest green eyes.

"It's all the tourists," I said, taking a cigarette from my pocket and placing it in my mouth, wishing I could light it. "They're too busy gawking at the lights on the buildings to watch for the lights on the road. Happens in every tourist trap. Heck, I'm surprised I made it this long without it happening." I watched her stare at the ceiling and I could feel a lump form in my throat. "But I'll make out okay."

She lowered her eyes then, and looked down at me. "But now you can't play the guitar," she said.

And she said it real simple. Matter of fact, like. And that lump in my throat dropped down to my chest. It hit me hard, like an anvil, and my heart started pounding.

"Damn," I whispered. "I hadn't thought of that till just now."

Lonnie kept staring at me. She shifted slightly but I was sort of staring off into space now. It was real quiet for a few minutes, and then she asked. "Are you okay?"

I didn't answer right away. But her question did snap me out of whatever I was starting to think, and I wondered what kind of look I had on my face. What was she seeing? "Yeah, I'm cool," I finally replied. "It ain't nothing to get down about, right?"

It looked like Lonnie was about to start crying. Like her eyes wanted to say something her mouth wouldn't speak. "That's a good philosophy," she said, with a little tear dripping down. It glistened on her skin, tracing a line down her cheek and curving around her earlobe to the back of her neck. I wanted to rub her earlobe between my fingers. "I wish I could think like that," she said, her voice cracking just a little bit.

I leaned back in the chair and crossed my legs. "Well, heck, Lonnie. There ain't nothing to it. You just have to go with the flow is all. Sometimes things happen that are outside your power. It's just one of those things there ain't no point in fighting, you know? You get sad when bad things happen, and you get happy when good things happen. The hell of it is, both good and bad are outside your power. It wasn't in your power being born, was it? I mean, you can look back on a thing... and you can maybe think of some decision you made that might have led to something else happening... maybe you stayed a bit longer after work one night, or maybe you decided to, I don't know, ignore the wrong person, or buy something you couldn't really afford... and maybe it seems like you may have brought something down on yourself… but all it is, is one decision coming from another decision that came from another decision and another and another that goes all the way back to the very beginning when you didn't have any kind of choice at all. So really… whatever happened to you, Lonnie… it wasn't really your f-fault. It wasn't your fault. Does that make any sense?"

She was really crying now. Not very loud, she was still trying to keep it in, but the tears were coming pretty strong. There was something graceful about it, the way she kept from losing herself in the tears. Like one of those war brides watching her man march off to war. And then she wiped her eyes, sniffled, and asked, "Do you know what happened to me?"

I took a deep breath and looked down at my boots. "Yeah, I heard some things," I sighed. "But I don't know what's for real from the bullshit."

"I must look pretty pathetic, huh?" she asked. And I was taken aback a bit by that.

"What do you mean?"

"I used to look down on girls that let this kind of thing happen to them. I mean, everyone told me this could be a dangerous city. My parents told me. My friends from school told me. I had a boyfriend all through high school, and I broke up with him to come here. I think he wanted to come with me, but I thought he was too small town… and I wanted to live in the big city. Because Las Vegas is where all the excitement is." Her words were sort of cracked, broken up by little whimpers. "I thought I was doing really good by not coming out here and becoming a stripper or something. I thought that was where all the girls went wrong out here. And now look at me. What kind of life is that where you think you're doing well just because you're not a stripper?"

I shook my head. "Ain't nothing pathetic about you, Lonnie. And, there ain't really nothing wrong with being a stripper either, really, I guess. I'm sure they're... all right as people. But I don't... I don't know."

She looked at me for a long time, and I kept hovering my head, trying to make myself hard to look at. I've always tried to avoid people staring at me. Feels like their taking aim at me or something. So I kept my eyes down, staring stupidly at my cast. My arm... all beat up to hell, and can't play the guitar. How do you like that?

"You want to know something funny?" she asked after a bit.

"Hmm?" I mumbled, keeping my head down.

"You're the only person I've talked to like this. Everyone else that has come by, I've just smiled and said how wonderful I am. I tell them not to worry about me, or make a fuss about anything. I don't know why. I guess I think I'm supposed to put a brave face on. But the truth is, I don't know if I'll ever not be afraid again. We really do live in a world of animals, don't we?"

I looked up then and stared at her face, at the way the pain and fear had soaked into her skin. And then I felt... I don't know. Kinda terrible. At this moment, I found her to be incredibly attractive. Sort of majestic. And then it came to me that this was another one of my problems. I guess I'm just attracted to the dramatic and the dysfunctional in a woman. Damned if they don't look amazing when they're angry or sad. I could see it now on Lonnie's face. If a woman looks good while she's crying, she's a good looking woman. However, all that she'd been through in the past couple days, while it may have added a glow to her features now, it was most certainly going to age her a little quicker. Kinda like... flying too close to the sun.

"I'm really tired," she said then. And I could see her struggling to keep her eyes open. "I know it sounds silly, Frank. But do you think you can sit here for a while. I'll sleep easier with a friend in the room."

"Keep away the nightmares, huh?" I said.

She smiled and nodded, and closed her eyes. She snuggled into her pillow and was out like a light. Just like that. It must have been some residual effect of the pain killers she was on. But I stayed where I was. And I watched the pulse in her neck and her eyelids fluttering. The lamplight reflected off her hair, and I watched.

After a while, I said, "I guess I've been running a little scared myself, Lonnie." She didn't respond, of course... and I probably wouldn't have said anything if she could. Sometimes it's a whole lot easier to get things off your chest that way. "As a matter of fact," I went on. "I think just about everything I've ever done has been because I was scared of something or other. Growing up, I was afraid of my father, my teachers, and getting in trouble. Hell, ever since I was a little kid, I've been running around trying not to get hurt or hurt myself. I was afraid of the bogyman until I was thirteen. Still kind of afraid of the dark."

I shook my head. What the hell was I doing? Hey man, I don't know why I did what I did. And I know it's easy to sympathize with certain people when the fact is I... well, maybe I'm just not very good at describing the reasons people deserve what happens to them. I'm not about to apologize or nothing. I trust my instincts enough to know better than that. I mean...

"To think I just stood there looking down the barrel of my own pistol, man. I mean, Lonnie, I didn't move a muscle. Can you understand what that felt like? Do you have any idea what kind of torture that is? Just being at someone else's mercy. Thinking they're gonna kill you and just waiting for that moment to come... and wondering what you can do about it, if anything. Just playing scenarios in your head about what in the world is possible for you at that moment... like, this is it! This is the end! And you're not moving a damn muscle to save yourself. Hell, I don't even know if I bust a sweat. I guess I can say at least I didn't piss myself. I guess I can have a shred of self-respect left for that. But, Jesus, what the hell is that good for? And now this," I motioned to the cast. "I can't even play the guitar now. It's like... I wonder if the coach was supposed to kill me, and because he didn't, the universe had to settle the account somehow. Instead of taking my life, it just took the only thing I'm good at. Now, I'm just, like, half dead. Or something."

Lonnie's mouth twitched and I shut up, thinking she might wake up again. I remained still while her lips puckered and then she made those smack-smack sounds with her mouth everybody makes in their sleep for some reason. Once she settled down again, I reached out and stroked her arm, from her elbow to her wrist. And then I clicked off the table lamp and left her alone.

# CHAPTER 11

ANYWAY, I'D HAD about enough of that shit. All that... sensitivity. I had to harden up quick if I wasn't going to lose my mind. It's amazing how adaptable a human being is. But you can teach them how to go without something way easier than how to handle too much.

I had to hitch a ride home on the bus because the caddy was impounded at the city yards. It would take a couple hundred bucks to get it out, and who knew how long that would take me to scrounge up. But anyway, sitting on that bus, I had me one of those moments of clarity. And I began to see my life like-- you know when you watch a movie, and the main character is a married guy, and they have a really beautiful actress play his wife, and you start to thinking the main character is bound to be a hero because he's one of those lucky people who's married to this incredibly beautiful woman, but the movie is supposed to be a serious drama and the main character is a down on his luck bum, and we're supposed to cheer for him to rise above some struggle... except meanwhile he's married to this really beautiful woman, the kind you *only* see in the movies, and she's way too beautiful for you to believe his character has any kind of real problems? Anyway, that's where I was at, man.

The bus didn't stop anywhere near my house, so I had to walk a good three miles the rest of the way home. It was a good walk. The sun was just beginning to set, and all the human garbage and scum I had to ride along with on the bus had put me on a natural high. By the time I reached my house, I just stood in the driveway, frozen, and I began to feel a little lucky for the first time in a long time. Maggie's Pontiac was still parked in the driveway under the tarp. The Coach had grabbed the kid, but forgot the car, sucker that he is. I couldn't help the smile on my face and rubbed the back of my neck. A cool breeze blew the bangs out of my eyes and I lit a cigarette. I stood there, smoking and laughing. Laughing for some damn reason I can't explain. But I laughed all the same.

The keys to the Pontiac were on the floor next to Maggie's open suitcase, under a pair of violet panties. I slipped the key ring around the thumb of my cast arm, and then rummaged through her suitcase until I found one of her bras. I stuffed the bra down my pants and then retrieved my .38 off the floor from where I'd kicked it last. I stuffed the .38 in my waistline and then stared at my shadow for a while, just breathing hard. I didn't have any ideas in my head. I was just, sort of on automatic. Like a wind-up toy that's been geared up to move around in circles. That's kinda what I felt like. Except I wasn't moving in circles. I was moving towards something else.

It's hard to tell what you're gonna do in any given situation. Even if you've done nothing but think about it for a real long time, maybe all your life. How many karate experts have you ever seen break out a roundhouse kick to finish a fight. That shit hardly ever happens. But people blow people away all the time, man. That's a fact.

I drove the Pontiac into town. It was getting on past midnight, so everything was just starting to pick up. I grabbed a bite to eat at a cheap Chinese restaurant and tried not to do what I thought I was going to do. I had to leave the .38 in the glove compartment and I was feeling jumpy. I kept imagining the Coach shuffling into the booth beside me. The bright red lamps hanging over every booth in the restaurant made me feel like I was sitting inside a microwave oven. I was seeing heat waves in front of me. I closed my eyes to calm myself down. *It's not going to do you any good freaking out, man.*

I guess I know myself pretty well. I think I always have. I think that's another one of my problems.

The better idea you have about yourself, the easier it is to put yourself on a path. Of course, that don't always mean you're going to be on the same path as everyone else, but hopefully you'll end up on the path you chose. I like to think all of my decisions are like a... like a vascular system. They have to come from the heart, man, and if they lead back to the heart, those are the decisions that really matter. Of course, I mean my real decisions in life, not all the shit I've done thanks to female or parental manipulation... or... or media brainwashing. That stuff... that's all just lead poisoning or something, or AIDS, or that stuff the Russian spies use to kill journalists. It's other people's decisions affecting you. That's the poisonous stuff. It's decisions coming from another person's heart, leading back to their heart… but they got bad hearts, man. And their decisions are poisoning your blood. That's the problem I'm aware of.

I'm aware of just how precisely other people are affecting me. And I'm pretty good at examining the decisions they made to do so. Of course, up till recently, I've let them get away with it. Like a damn four-eyed geek lettin' himself get bullied in the locker room. Just sittin' there sniveling, cryin' while the other kids laugh at him. It's enough to make you hate yourself. What kind of piece of shit can't defend himself?

Well, I ain't some four-eyed pecker, man. It was time to resolve a few things. If you catch my drift.

I slid into the Pontiac, belched up some wonton or some shit, and drove straight to Mitch's place.

There was a new band up on stage. Playing some god-awful racket with… motherfuckin' three lead guitars. Jesus Christ, man. Can you believe it? People don't get enough distraction from their lives with television and video games, they gotta go and be distracted beyond all sense by the live talent? I tried to wipe the sneer off my face, forced my way through the crowd and found a place to lean against the wall. The reverberations of the bass drum through the cheap wood paneling nearly stopped my heart. Music used to mean something. It was the sound of a people. And shit, I guess it still is. Take a listen some time and you'll find I've been right about everything all along.

I was glad to see none of my old backing band was playing with these clowns. I don't know what I would've done if they had been. And then I started to feel my anger rising up again. This was the shit Mitch wanted instead of me.

*Hell with it.*

I worked my way to the bar, taking advantage of the undulations of the audience to grab some ass and jab a few kidneys. When I finally sidled up to the bar, I held my hand up to get the bartender's attention. And of course it was that whore, Mona. Probably working a double shift just to be there to piss me off. I smiled.

"Get me a cold one, beautiful," I said.

"Oh, don't you get me all flustered," she smiled in return, and brought me my beer. "Can't stay away, huh?"

*Why you sarcastic cunt, I will fuck you to death!*

"Can't stay away from you, hot stuff."

She giggled and went back to work with one of those fake ass hand nods. The man sitting next to me tipped his beer at me in salute, as if he was impressed I knew her. And that irked me too. But I guess if his ears liked this music, his eyes probably saw Mona as the Taj Mahal. I lit a cigarette and made my way to Mitch's office.

He was doing a bump with a couple of girls and hadn't even bothered to close his door. I walked right in and slapped him on the shoulder. He jumped halfway out of his chair but quickly recovered himself.

"Aw, shit, Frank! How you been, man? How long's it been?"

"Just since earlier this week, my boy," I said, smiling and smiling and smiling.

"Well, hell, come on in, man, come on in," he waved his arms in wide circles, and whether he meant the girls to make room for me to sit or not, that's how it worked out. I sat down in front of the desk and waved away his offering of coke. "Okay, okay," he said, wobbling his head like an idiot, showing off for the girls. "A-jibber-jab-jab-jabber!"

I sort of jumped back in my chair at that, and tried not to look too crazy eyed at him. The girls just laughed. Eating it up, man. Like they always do in those situations. I wondered if Lonnie had been the same way.

I stared at the girls, from one to the other, trying to figure out which one was the better looking. I hesitated to pick a favorite, because as soon as I found one prettier, I'd get all upset she was there to begin with, and I'd start thinking what a tragedy it is that her life led her to Mitch's presence... and what the hell was she missing at home to make her feel the way she was spending the evening right now was so much better than some other, more wholesome, way. Damn! There was a dark haired girl and a brunette and I think the dark haired girl was definitely the prettier one. By a mile, man. Just fantastic.

Mitch must have caught me looking because he sort of did a double take and then stared right at the dark haired girl. "Kayla, show Frank your titties," he said. And sure enough she did.

She pulled her shirt down slowly, so that the tight material pressed against the soft flesh, molding it like

143

a gentle wave until the nipple popped out. I stared, of course, trying not to look like I was.

"Oooohwheee!" Mitch said, or something like that.

Kayla laughed like she thought Mitch was the funniest guy in the world. And she looked right at me and smiled. The brunette laughed too and, probably afraid she was being ignored reached over and cupped Kayla's left breast and jiggled it. Kayla's laugh turned into a sort of kitty cat moan and her wide eyes narrowed at me as she pinched her nipple tight.

"Whatsa matter, Frank? High blood pressure?" Mitch asked, laughing. And I didn't know what he was talking about until I tasted the blood on my tongue. Another damn nose bleed. I froze, afraid of making too big a deal of it. But it didn't seem to bother the girls none. Kayla leaned over and rubbed her finger on my top lip. She held the finger in front of me, with a small smear of my blood on the very tip of her painted nail, and then stuck the finger in her mouth, sucked on it like it was… well.

My whole body was vibrating. Shivering.

Then she took my hand and played with my fingers. She looked down at it as if she were intensely fascinated by it. As if she were an alien and had never seen an appendage with its structure. She rubbed the back of my hand with her own, played with the webbing between my fingers, and then placed my hand on her breast. The brunette giggled and Mitch made some kind of silly noise, his eyes bugging out of his head. I felt goose bumps rise on her warm flesh under my sweaty palm as I squeezed. I then slowly ran my hand down her torso. Feeling the ridges of her ribs and firmness of her belly. I slowly circled her belly button with the tip of my finger. I looked at her.

"It's hard to believe," I said, lifting my hand and holding the index finger two inches from my thumb. "That when you were this big, your ma and pa were thinking about what they were going to call you. How could they vocalize all the love and hope and… optimism they felt with your arrival in the world? And they came up with Kayla, huh Kayla?"

And then the brunette finally said something. She said, "Are you a fag, or somethin'?"

"Me? Hell no. I was just wondering what leads two girls like you to this… whatever this is."

Kayla's smile shrank just a little bit. Probably because she wasn't catching my drift. With that confusion was captured something I've always found intoxicating in women. The way her mouth froze in an uncertain smile made my heart melt. And all I could imagine was the heartbreak her parents would feel if they could see her now. And God help them if they wouldn't be heartbroken about it. And then I thought of Lonnie again. I lost my erection.

"Hey, how would you girls like to know you're partying with a guy who put the last girl he was with in the hospital?" I said, abruptly, still smiling.

It took a few seconds for Mitch to work that out. And then his eyes really bulged out. He leaned forward and put his hands on the desk, his fingers spread wide. "Frank. Whoa!" he exclaimed. His mouth looped like a howling wolf the way he overemphasized the 'whoa', his head shaking from right to left.

I smiled and put a cigarette to my mouth with my cast hand. My other hand was on Kayla's thigh. I put the cigarette between my teeth, still smiling.

"Hey, Mitch. Just kidding," I said, giggled a bit and looked at Kayla and the brunette. "But not really. He did a number on her, let me tell you."

"Frank!" Mitch shouted, and added with a nervous sort of laugh. "What are you doin', buddy?"

I looked right at him. Maybe I wasn't smiling anymore, but it felt like I was. "May even have raped her. But we're not too clear on that, are we?"

The girls didn't know what to think, and Kayla had lost that adorable confused smile. But she was still a looker. Probably better looking than any woman I've ever been with.

"Frank, I told you, man, I didn't touch her, man. I already talked to the cops and everything." He giggled again. "Now, c'mon. You're gonna bust up the party."

"I liked her, Mitch. Did you know that? I liked her." Another look at the girls. "Her name was Lonnie. Lonnie Higgins." I looked back at Mitch and slammed my cast arm on his desk. "Lonnie!" I shouted, my voice cracking.

Mitch pushed back in his chair, but if he was thinking about coming back at me, he quickly changed his mind when I pulled the .38.

"Oh, Jesus, God," he said with the gun barrel closing a nostril.

The brunette screamed and Kayla just stared with wide eyes. I reached back and forced the office door shut, closing the four of us off from the rest of the bar. Though I could still feel and hear the thumping from the… music.

"I never knew you had a thing for her, Frank," Mitch jabbered, all his words running together. "Jesus, if I'd known I wouldn't have gone near her, I swear."

"So you admit it, huh? Finally."

"No! No, Frank. I swear to God I didn't beat up on her. It wasn't me. It wasn't, Jesus."

"I guess it felt pretty good to beat up on a poor little defenseless girl, eh, you mother fucker? I guess you didn't think anybody'd come to collect, huh? Like she wasn't worth a damn. And you!" I shouted, turning the gun on the brunette. "Suck on her titties or I'll shoot you in the face. Call me a fag, will you, god damn it?"

Her face distorted by fear, the brunette bent down as if her body were slowly freezing solid and pushed her mouth against Kayla's breast. I watched in silence for, I don't know, a few seconds, before finding the stiff motions of her tongue utterly disgusting, and then turned back to Mitch, who hadn't moved an inch even with the gun pointed away from him. "I can't believe you did it, Mitch," I said. "Just tell me why?"

Mitch raised his hands in the air, as if I were a cop who had told him to freeze. "I didn't do anything," he said, and repeated. "I- didn't- do- anything."

*Yes you did, Mitch. You're just too stupid to get it.*

"I saw her today, Mitch. At the hospital. She says it was you."

I could see the fright, fear and betrayal in his eyes. I kind of felt sorry for him. Well, I guess. It's always hard to learn someone you cared about has turned their back on you. Maybe the hardest thing in the world. And you would think after it's happened time after time, that you'd get used to it. That it wouldn't hurt so much after a while. But then, it always seems to hurt worse. Just like with me and my ex. But, even then, I think I would've taken it better if I hadn't seen the videos.

I reached back and whacked Mitch upside the head with the gun. He bounced back in his seat, but I hadn't hit him that hard. Just enough to stun him a bit. He shut his eyes tight and brought his hands up to cover his face as if he was afraid I was going to hit him again. Kayla let out a yelp, like a lost puppy begging shelter, and the brunette was crying. Tears ran down in rivulets over her cheeks and down to her lips where they met with the saliva of her tongue as it did awkward, mechanic circles around Kayla's pink areola.

"What the hell you crying for?" I asked her. "You scared of me or something?" I laughed, motioned to Mitch. "He's the guy you need to be afraid of. I'm the guy defending you bitches."

Kayla's teeth were clenched tight, and I can only assume she was trying not to freak out. She was doing a pretty good job considering. I stared down at the back of the brunette's swiveling head. As much as I thought I'd like to see her face on a titty, I couldn't help but feel a little disgusted. It was all so phony and demeaning. How can this stuff turn anybody on, man?

"Alright, that's enough of that shit," I said, nudging the brunette on the shoulder. "You girls go on and cover yourselves up for Christ's sake. It's like the damn... fall of Babylon in here." I turned my attention back to Mitch. His arms had begun to lower, but as soon as he caught my eye he lifted them back up. "Okay, Mitch. I might be a sonuvabitch, but I'm inclined to believe you. Maybe you didn't beat up on Lonnie, after all."

He sighed visibly and then lowered his arms again. "I've been tryin' to tell you, Frank. Jesus. Hell, man, I've already been cleared by the police. And that detective guy who came snooping around. I've been through the ringer, man. I ain't lying."

"Detective? Like a private detective?"

"Well, shit. Yeah, detective Bollinger, or Blansky. Didn't he speak to you, too?"

*Aw, hell.*

"What would a private detective want to speak to me about?"

Mitch gave an exaggerated shrug. "Fuck if I know, man. I thought they were talking to everybody Lonnie knew. I thought maybe they suspected you, man."

I chuckled. "Man, that's just crazy, Mitch."

"Well, you know," he shrugged again.

*Yeah, I know.*

Kayla and the brunette had backed each other into the corner of the office, which fine by me. At least they'd stopped their crying. I stuck the .38 back into my pocket.

"What did the guy look like?" I asked, then. "The detective." Though I already knew.

"Looked like a million other guys," Mitch said. "Blonde, grayish hair. Blue eyes. Looked kinda square. Like an insurance salesman or something."

I looked down at the floor. There were old coffee and mildew stains on every tile. I had a feeling if I stared hard enough I'd see something like my future in 'em. And I asked Mitch real quietly, "What was his whole name?"

"I don't remember. But I got his card somewhere in my desk."

I realized he was asking permission so I gave a nod. He opened the top desk drawer, the long thin one filled with paper clips and pens. He found the business card under a pile of receipts and handed it to me. I watched the hand with the card in it come closer, like it was the sun coming up slowly over the Spring Mountains. I took the card out of his hand, looked down at it and stifled a chuckle.

"Art Blansky," I read the name aloud, then looked back at the girls. "Don't it figure?" I asked.

# CHAPTER 12

HONESTY IS PRETTY important. I can admit I'm not always the most honest person. But I think I've been pretty honest, with myself, at least. And I know enough about myself to realize that my life has been one long revenge fantasy. There's just no way around that. Of course, I'd like it to be different. But then I go and fantasize about getting revenge on the things that kept it from being any different. And then I'm stuck in one of those vicious cycles. And it's just something I dwell on. It's really too bad. Because I think I could've been a pretty good, honest, productive human being if I'd been given the right breaks. But, I guess a whole lotta other people can say the same thing. Not that that matters any, though. Least, not the way I have to look at it. The problem with holding a grudge is you're always having to reposition the memories related to it. You're always having to put it in a different perspective. Like, say, a bad break-up from way back in junior high. It crushed you for a few years, but once you hit your twenties, that grudge just kinda gets shuffled into the experience box. Same with spankings and whatnot. After a while, you have to forget the humiliation and remember the lesson. You don't stay angry at the stove for burning your hand. Do you? I sure don't. But, yeah. It took me a while. When I was a little bitty boy, I used to think the entire household was out to get me. The stove was too hot and the fridge was too cold.  A can of green beans could split your wig, and your own daddy pushes you around.  It's just a whole lot better to be a grown-up, that's for sure.  At least you know, if you're smart... you know what can hurt you... and why.  And... in some ways... you can choose just how much you're gonna let someone hurt you.

Another thing I realized, is once you get on the road to killing someone... you'll realize that you've been on that road your entire life.

I drove around for a real long time.  Whenever I hit a red light I checked out the business card I'd taken from Mitch.  I don't know if I was expecting it to say something different every time I looked at it or what, but no, it stayed the same.  There was no address listed on the card but there was the name of an office building.  I knew the building and so drove over to it and parked outside of the suite listed.  I stared up at the ceiling of the Pontiac for a few seconds, staring at the dome light, before realizing I wasn't in my Caddy convertible.  I got out, sat down on the hood and lit a cigarette, shivering at the early morning chill.

Art Blansky's name was stenciled on the door under the name of the agency he worked for.  There was one name above his and a few underneath.  I exhaled a lungful of smoke and watched it drift.  I was depressed.  The son of a bitch actually was a private detective.  I didn't want to believe it but it was true.

I tossed my cigarette, lit another and stared up at the sky.  It was getting up around sunset.  The moment when the sky turns from black to blue, but the stars still shine through.  I've always found it beautiful...

that short moment when the earth sees the sun right before it rises over the mountains to fuck everything up. And before the heat comes, there's that blast of wind being driven before it, blowing all the dust and old newspapers out of the street. A lot of people don't notice things like that. I wondered if Art Blansky ever noticed it.

The little detail of his being a private detective made me want to lose my lunch. It's hard to explain, I guess, but… well, it made me feel a little like maybe he was the star of the movie that my life had become. When I was younger, I always fantasized about becoming a private detective. Like Humphrey Bogart. If Art Blansky had been a police detective I wouldn't have minded all that much. But a private detective, man. That was impressive. He probably had a tough childhood. An interestingly failed marriage with a woman who still loved him but couldn't take the hard life of a Detective's wife. Probably a war veteran, or something or other. Maybe a Green Beret. Shit. That would just make me the bad guy. Not even the main bad guy, just some piece of shit he got to act tough on. Like Dirty Harry with one of the shitty back alley muggers. And he did. He was cool about it, too. All filled with confidence. He got to have it because I didn't have it.

But get a load of this, man. While I waited, I looked down at my pack of cigarettes and read the logo with the Latin words in a banner. I don't read Latin, but I think I've heard somewhere that it says something about reaching for the stars. I might be wrong about that, but I don't think I am. Anyhow, it made me wonder if it's always the best thing to do. Shoot for the stars, I mean. One time I took a bath and drowned a flea that had hopped from my dog to me. Now, you might figure the flea was just a stupid insect. But I figure, maybe the flea was just tired of the dog and wanted something better. Maybe all the fleas on a dog just wish they were on something else, man. Like it or not, Chief, that flea was just shooting for the stars.

I got back into the car and closed my eyes. What the hell was I doing there, man? I could be in my own bed, wrapped in my own covers... not covered by early morning moisture. There were all kinds of things rushing through my head, and then again, nothing. I fell asleep anyway.

The sun was well up by the time I opened my eyes. I don't know if maybe it was a car horn that woke me up, or if it was just fate. I yawned, stretched a little bit and wiped the sleep out of my eyes. Then saw Art Blansky crossing the parking lot through the sun flare off the windshield.

I hunched down behind the wheel, praying like hell he didn't walk directly past the Pontiac on his way to the office. He didn't. And I don't think he noticed me. He reached his office, unlocked the door and squinted into the sun once before going inside. I realized my heart was beating fast and my muscles were all tingly. I rammed my fist down on my thigh- a little too hard- but it served to wake me up. After a while, with Blansky not coming out of the office, I managed to calm down. I stared at the door. Lit another cigarette.

"Blansky," I said aloud. He even had the perfect private detective name.

Shit man. Who was I fooling? I wasn't going to do anything to hurt this man. If anything, what with his awesome name, cool demeanor, and Green Beret training... he would be the one to hurt me. Maybe even kill me this time. And if this were a movie, right now would be when he did it. And I guess I would deserve it, being the lily livered jerk I'd been lately. I could just go home. Forget about all of this. The humiliation. The frustration. There was no need for any more regrets. I could just start over. Become a fat Elvis. Start packing on the pounds. Eat gravy shakes and tons of mayonnaise. Go to bed, wake up tomorrow and look for another job. It wasn't really all that difficult. Millions of people did it every day. Millions.

Jesus Christ, man, there's always a choice---

Blansky tapped on the window. The ring on his pinky clinked against the glass and he smiled real big at me. "Roll it down, brother," he said, his voice muffled by the window.

I rolled it down a crack, stared out.

"How about a smoke?" he asked.

I pushed a cigarette through the crack.

He took it, stuck it between his teeth. "Thanks," he said, lighting it. He puffed on it to get it going, took a long drag, inhaled, stared off into space while he exhaled, and then said, "Come on into the office, Frank. It's too damn hot out here."

I stared, watched him walk back into his office without ever looking back to see if I was coming. I gripped the steering wheel and, though it could have been my imagination, heard the keys jingle, prompting me to turn the ignition and get the hell out of there. But something was making me hesitate. I don't know what. I guess I figured it would be, I don't know... rude if I left. It's always been hard for me to refuse a request. It's one of the reasons I hate homeless people, holding up their signs at every street corner.

It looked like a place they sell car insurance. There was one private room toward the back, but the other detective's, including Blansky's were situated in small cubicles. There was a ding-dong sound as I stepped over the black mat by the door, and I stood in the doorway until the echo faded away. I stared at the long line of cubicle partitions as if it were the beginnings of an intricate maze I'd been coerced into, like a rat, by Blansky's beckoning arm. His arm stuck out from one of the middle cubicles, a powder blue sport coat with a meaty hand waving me on. I approached slowly, my hands slipped into my back pockets, and stretched my neck to see into the cubicle, only slightly prepared for imminent violence. Blansky sat in a swivel chair in front of a cheaply made faux wood desk and I leaned against the edge partition.

"Have a seat, Frank," he said, indicating a non-swivel chair on the opposite side of the desk, exactly as if I were there to buy insurance.

"I'm alright to stand," I said.

Blansky didn't immediately respond. He swiveled a bit in the chair, his legs wide apart, almost as if he was begging me to kick him in the balls. Every second I didn't was a small victory for him. The slight grin on his face was proof of that. He was reading me like a book. That's the most insulting thing of all, man.

"That chair ain't gonna break your legs, Frank," he said, still motioning at the chair.

"I do hope not," I said, trying to smile. I continued to stand.

Blansky huffed a short laugh. "Okay, Frank. I get it. I understand." He swiveled toward the desk and spoke facing away from me. "I was just trying to get you comfortable. Seeing as how you are the one who came to see me. I just thought you'd like to take a seat and have an actual conversation with me, Frank. I mean, that is what you were waiting around out front of my office for, right, Frank?"

I sat down.

He smiled, then opened the top drawer of his desk and came out with a bag of corn nuts. He kept smiling as he popped a small handful into his mouth and stared at me as he chewed, loudly and slowly. After he swallowed, he motioned at my cast. "What's the story with that?" he asked.

"Wild dog," I replied.

"You got good instincts. Best way to defend against a wild bitch is to stuff your arm right down its mouth."

"Obviously."

He smiled again, popped another handful. "I guess you're a little sore with me, huh. What can I say? I sometimes can't control my anger. That's on me,

Frank. I suppose I didn't stop to think how that might affect you."

I guess he was talking about having jabbed the gun in my face.

He went on. "It's the job, though. It's what I get paid to do."

"I thought private detectives just hung out in alleys, took pictures and shit."

"Oh, I do that, too."

I reached back to scratch under my shoulder blade. To my surprise, Blansky's eyes shone a little nervous. And I started to think a little deeper. Blansky did not know how I found out about him. I think it was making him doubt his first impression of me.

"Maggie's husband paid you to wave a gun in my face?" I asked.

Blansky's jaw muscles tensed. "Frank... some people... they don't actually have to pay to get things done. You catch my drift? Some people... they know what they want and... well, one way or another they're gonna get it."

"You did it for free then?"

He wasn't smiling anymore. "Naw, Frank. It weren't free."

"What then?"

Blansky leaned forward. I could tell he was getting impatient. "The man wanted his son back, Frank. And, yeah, he wanted to be sure you weren't porkin' his wife, but that was secondary. As far as he is concerned, you're just some man who helped to kidnap his boy." He laughed. "You really shouldn't have made those phone calls, though. Ha! A fucking ransom." He calmed down. "But seriously. I know that was all bullshit. You ain't no kidnapper, that's obvious." He tilted the bag of corn nuts up, emptying it into his mouth. He crunched and chewed, with both cheeks filled to puffing out until gradually lessening as the morsel were devoured, he swallowed and took a breath. The smell of the chips wafted throughout the cubicle. "You sure did beat hell out of that girl, though," he said then, sort of off the cuff.

I stared silently for what seemed like an hour, surprisingly, straight into his eyes. "What the fuck did you just say to me?" I asked, feeling an intense, but subdued anger... like anger was a television program I knew was on the next station over... but I hadn't reached it yet. It's a silly metaphor but an honest one.

"Oh, I think you know," he said, tossed the empty snack bag at a trash can in the corner, missed, and then slid a photograph across the desk at me. "Heh. Don't get your panties in a bunch, Frank. I ain't exactly judging you."

I stared at the photograph. It was a picture of a woman. The entire left side of her face was swollen to about three times normal size. The swelling closed the left eye, and the entire region around the socket was a sickly pale color compared to the dark red and purple surrounding it. Blood smeared from her temple down to her neck, spattering the collar of her ripped shirt.

"Looks kinda like the Elephant Man, don't it?" Blansky chuckled.

"Who is it?" I asked.

"Oh, come one, Frank. Don't be that guy today. That's Lonnie Higgins."

He chuckled again and took the photograph back, stared at it, himself, and then said, "It's a damn shame. She was a pretty girl. Looked like a damn centerfold from the nineties." He looked up at me and shrugged. "Why couldn't you beat up the ugly ones, eh, Frank?"

My leg began to shake uncontrollably, and I tried to weight it with my cast arm. "You're crazy," I said. "I didn't do that to Lonnie. I wouldn't do that." There was a buzzing in my head. Rhythmic. The longer I was in the office, its pitch began to shift, and pretty soon I was hearing the King himself. Good old Elvis Aaron. My hands are shaky and my knees are weak. And God help me, I started imagining Blansky as one of those Fat Elvis' everybody seems to love. Sitting in front of me with the lights gleaming off the sequins on his sleeves, the cape draped over one shoulder, a diamond tipped cane cradled in his elbow the way girls hold their school books.

"Sure you did it," he smiled. "And I'm willing to bet my right nut she isn't your first. Oh, but don't worry, Frank. It ain't my case. I mean, not in an official sense. I haven't been hired by anybody or anything. No sir, it's more a curiosity I have. Like reading a mystery novel. Sometimes I just gotta know whodunit."

"But that wasn't me. So you might want t-to keep looking," I tried to smile.

He ignored me, just kept on talking. "It's funny how these things have a habit of coming together.

Just the day before old sweet tits Maggie's husband, Roger hired me to find you, I was reading about Miss Lonnie Higgins in the paper. It didn't take much to figure out it was you after I started looking into it. I mean, I'm trying to figure out why you'd kidnap a little boy and then I find out you used to work with the girl who got attacked. So... "

"So what do you think is going to happen to Maggie now that her old man's got her back?" I blurted out, desperate to steer the conversation back to where I'd wanted it at the beginning.

It took Blansky a moment to adjust to the question. "What do you mean?"

"Well, she cut off his hand. I don't imagine they'll be renewing their vows anytime soon."

"Stranger things have happened. And, Frank, do you really think I'd reunite a woman with a man who was out to hurt her? I'm sure they're having a pleasant time at their hotel on the strip. Least they were last time I saw them." That damn smile kept creeping back. "But there you go again, making me forget who I'm talking to. As if you care about a woman getting her head bashed in."

I took a deep breath. "I told you I didn't do that to Lonnie. I loved that girl," I hissed.

Blansky stared, clenched his teeth. "Not anymore?" he asked, jabbing his finger over the photograph.

I stumbled. "W-well... I don't know."

"I guess she never will get those looks back."

"She'll just have to learn to lean on some other attribute, I guess," I said.

He started to laugh again. I reached out and grasped a handful of his hair before he could, and smashed his head down on the desk. I was elated to find his hair had not been a toupee. His body went into a rigid spasm, his back arching and I held onto the back of his neck, pushing and rubbing his face across the desk. He kicked his leg back swiftly, and I had to hop out of the way. I could tell he was trying to hook my leg with his own to knock me off balance, and as I shifted to avoid that, he slipped out of my grip, swung around wildly and lurched at me. I raised my arm to cover my face, anticipating a right cross, but he landed a punch at my chest. Nothing debilitating, but enough to make me cough. He tried to follow up with an upper cut to my gut, but I managed to sidestep it. I swung my cast arm down, just barely grazed his forehead, and felt his body tackle into me. He forced my back against the desk and started ramming my ribs with his fists. I yelped audibly, lifted my legs and squeezed his torso, constricting his movements enough that he stopped hitting me and tried to pry my legs apart. I hit him hard with my good hand. He used one arm to fend me off, like he was swatting a fly, while continuing to try and pry my legs loose with the other. Then I bashed his face with the cast. He ignored it at first, but then blood began to spray from a deep cut over his eye.

"Mother fucker!" he screamed, then grabbed me by the ears and smashed his head into my face. There was a split second of bright white light, another split second of pure black. I opened my eyes, feeling dizzy and found that he'd freed himself from my leg lock. Before I could latch back on, he tugged at my jacket, pulling it up over my head, trying to wrap me up in it. I yelled and rolled myself across the desk. I hit the floor and jumped back up. The desk was between us... but not for long. Blansky grabbed the corner and flipped it up on its side. It crashed against the partition, falling into the adjoining cubicle. As he came at me, he blocked the punches I threw with my good hand, came in with his own jab that almost connected with my throat. My eyes began to water and I almost felt like crying.

He grabbed me by the neck and forced me against the underside of the desk. The legs jabbed into my shoulder blades. I couldn't feel his punches, but I could tell my head was rocking back and forth with each hit. I saw him reel back for another big left hook and moved out of the way as quickly as possible. His fist slammed hard into the metal desk and I bashed him again with my cast. His nose burst at the bridge and blood came flooding out. He screamed something at me, blood dripping into his mouth, painting his teeth red. I swung him around, using the momentum to trip him to the ground, then forced my full weight on top of him. I hammered my cast into his face and head until the blood soaked it the whole way round.

I lost count of how many times I hit him, but I kept hitting him until well after he'd stopped struggling. I got up, bracing myself on my knees to catch my breath. I saw the photograph of Lonnie Higgins in the corner of my eye, scattered with the other papers and documents that had been in his desk. I reached over with a groan, grabbed the photograph, crumpled it and then stuffed it in Blansky's mouth. Some of my own blood dripped down on his face, mixed with his own. I found it funny.

# CHAPTER 13

WHATEVER BONE HAD broken in my arm felt like it broke all over again. It felt like my entire forearm was blowing up like a damn balloon of blood and shit pressing against the cast. I slumped down in Blansky's chair, lit a cigarette and swiveled. A pop machine in the lobby hummed loudly and clicked when the compressor shut on, and I jumped thinking someone was coming through the door. But nobody came. Maybe they pulled rotating shifts, man. I don't know. Either way I had the place more or less to myself. The blood on my mouth kept drying on the cigarette butt, tearing small layers off my bottom lip every time I took a drag, but I was enjoying that cigarette, man. I guess Blansky wasn't much special after all. I looked down at his body without looking at his head, tried to smile but stopped 'cause it hurt. I ran my fingers over my face, feeling all the welts and soft spots. The bastard had made a bad orange out of me.

After a while, I flipped the desk right ways up, careful not to drop it on Blansky, and rifled through the drawers to find a clue as to which hotel Roger was holding Maggie and Sam hostage. It took a while but I eventually found it. Now all I had to do was drive down there and save the day. I took a long drag on the cigarette and blew the smoke straight up, imagining my life in black and white. Sitting in Blansky's chair, at Blansky's desk... it felt like I belonged there, man. All I was missing was the whatchacallit, the hat, a fedora. And a long raincoat. Blansky didn't have any of that. But Blansky wasn't the star of the show. Not anymore, anyway. I snuffed the cigarette out on the armrest and flicked the butt down at Blansky. "Something to remember me by," I said in my best Elvis, and laughed.

I hopped back in the Pontiac and checked the time on the dash clock. Traffic on the strip is always high, but I sure didn't want to go riding around at lunch time. It was 10:00. Not so bad.

Blansky's office was in the old town, so it took about forty-five minutes in traffic to reach the main strip. I parked in one of the cheap lots, not wanting to dodge pedestrians the rest of the way to the hotel, and walked from there. I got a few stares, I guess on account of my busted face, but I think I got a few more thanks to my cast now being a very dark pink color. It made me a little self-conscious. Some things get stared at for a reason, man. And for the first time, I guess, I could understand why people were staring. Walking around with your arm wrapped in a pink cast is kinda like walking around with an umbrella when it ain't raining, or shoes with no socks; it just seems kinda faggy. After a while, I took my jacket off and draped it over my arm. I held my hand over my face to smoke and swerved around the tourists, sluts and cock suckers, stopped to stare at the tigers for a spell.

I bent over and hawked a blood gobbed loogie into a trash can, braced myself against the wall for a while before continuing on. Nobody noticed, so I guess it was alright. The pain in my arm was weighing on me, spreading like a fire across the upper half of my torso. I grit my teeth and stumbled on, leaning a bit to the side, jerking one foot in front of the other until finally reaching the hotel. I entered the casino and walked as fast as I could to the slots where I collapsed. I looked around, opening my eyes wide and breathing heavy. Luckily there weren't very many people around so I didn't have to worry about making a scene. There were a few old guys in the row across from me, retirees with hearing aids and compression socks happy to spend their remaining days shucking away one coin after the other. I fumbled in my pocket for some change but all the machines nearby only accepted tokens. I got up, swallowed hard and walked over to the token machine. I put in a ten and got back five tokens, then head back to the slot. On the way, I grabbed a coin bucket and vomited into it. I slumped down in the seat, wiped my forehead and sighed. Now I was starting to feel better. One of the old guys craned his neck and sneered, the old fuck. But I guess I'd be grumpy too if I had to witness another man's salad days. Heh-heh.

I lit a cigarette, let the smoke fill my lungs and refresh the acidic taste in my mouth. I put a token into the slot and pulled the lever. While the reels spun round, I caught my reflection in the glass. It wasn't as bad as I imagined it to be. As a matter of fact, it did my lip some good. It was puffed up to the side, just like Elvis. Some of the other swelling must have gone down already, and I'd never been one to bruise, so it wasn't so bad. Not bad at all.

The reels came to a sudden stop- two lemons and a… like a fucking hot dog or something- and I got four tokens out of it.

"Hey," I said, you know, kinda excited.

I put another token in, pulled the lever.

Three hot dogs, man!

The machine spat out tokens. Thirty-five of them. I leaned over, poured my vomit out of the coin bucket into the coin tray of the machine next to mine, and then scooped my winnings into the bucket.

I put in another token.

One cherry, two lemons, only three tokens.

"Hmm," I sighed. It was a win, but… still.

I gave it another go.

Three cherries! Twenty-five tokens.

"My boy, my boy!"

One more time!

I noticed the old man sneer again. "Hey, fuck you, man," I said to him, and pulled the lever.

One hot dog, one peach and a cowboy hat. Damn.

Another wave of dizziness swept over me. My head thumped against the machine, and I stayed there with my eyes closed, letting the cool metal soothe me. I opened one eye and rolled it to see the old man still staring at me. "Whatsamatter, Chief?" I mumbled. "You still raw you helped the wrong side win the war?"

I chuckled and he sneered some more, scrunching up his face like a hand puppet before finally taking his old ass the hell away from me. The few old people sitting in the same line as him watched him hobble away, and I wondered what was going through their minds. I suppose they were filled with thoughts about how guys like me were destroying society or something along those lines. Which really was too bad. Because there's no way to convince them they're wrong, man. They won't ever take the responsibility, themselves. They're like children that way. But you know how it is, man. The circle of life. Born into diapers and dying that way. God help 'em.

I felt my strength return, grabbed by bucket of winnings and stepped away from the slots. I was able to walk in a relative straight line to the payout desk to exchange the tokens, got the cash and then went to the restroom fast as I could.

Thankfully, there was nobody else in there. I rested my elbows on the counter and splashed water on my face and the back of my neck. I tried to rinse the blood out of the cast, but that wasn't happening. I could barely feel my hand now; and that just a slight tingle. I thumped it on the counter and let out a small cry of frustration. If I could just break the damn thing off… let my skin breath, maybe it would feel better. I was sure my circulation was all kinds of screwed up. What if a blood clot formed? People die from stuff like that. I've heard of people dying from lying in bed too long because a blood clot blocked the flow of blood from their legs. Jesus Christ, man. I once knew someone who claimed their husband died because a piece of plaque worked its way from his tooth to his brain. Plaque, man. I tell you, I sometimes wonder if we're not from this Earth. It seems everything on it is trying to kill us. Maybe all the mammals are from space, or something, and, I don't know… like the Scientologist's are right, right? And somehow we adapted the best we could, but…well, we got lucky because all the probiotics decided to help us out. And so we got all these tiny aboriginal microbes fighting a war inside our bodies. Some trying to kill us, others trying to save us… and maybe whichever side is winning is what makes us act the way we do.

The bathroom attendant stared impatiently at me, holding a thick paper towel out for me. I stared back at him, water dripping from my face and hands.

"You been here the whole time, man?" I asked.

"A lot of people miss the urinal, kid," he answered. "Just take it easy out there."

I looked down to see I'd pissed all over the floor. Like a damn animal. "Yes, sir," I said, clearing my throat. I handed him a dollar. He took it with a polite bow and let go of the towel, then sat back down on his black stool, stared straight ahead as I dried myself off.

"How do you do it, man?" I asked. "It's like a… like a magic trick."

His mustache curled at the sides as he smiled, and he spread his hands apart.

"Yeah, I got you," I said, handing him a couple more bucks.

He tossed me a mint and a vial of aspirin. "Looks like you can use it," he said with a wink.

I made my way to the elevators. I had to get to Maggie and Sam quick before I lost it completely. Something was wrong with me. There was no denying it. I was rambling. Probably talking to myself. Or maybe not. The couple in the car with me didn't seem bothered. But still, I guess Blansky got a few too many good hits in.

There was a *ding* sound and the elevator came to a stop. I smiled at the couple as they made their exit, then pressed the *close doors* button furiously. The elevator continued to climb until coming to a stop on the twenty-ninth floor where I got out. Blansky's file had Roger staying in suite 5616. I consulted the diagram next to the elevator to see which direction to take, and then made my way toward it. I approached the suite, feeling my adrenaline pitch with every step closer. My heart pounded, I could hear the blood in my ears, and I walked straight past suite 5616 to the end of the hall. I turned the corner and tried to calm myself down. I stood up straight, resting my fists on my hips and took a long, deep breath. I had to remind myself, I did in fact have options. I could call down to the lobby and have Roger paged. I could pull the fire alarm. Or, I could do what I was good at, *wrap your shirt around your face and knock on the door.*

Turns out, I didn't have to do anything. As I peeked my head around the corner I saw Sam and Maggie step out of the suite and head down the hall toward the elevators. I gasped and blinked a couple times to make sure I wasn't seeing things. I waited a few seconds to make sure Roger wasn't going to come out, and then skipped after them. I barely reached the elevator in time, skid past the closing doors and smacked right into Maggie, pressing her against the mirrored wall.

She let out a high pitched yelp and gave me the crazy eyes before recognizing it was me. We were flat up against each other like a couple of flapjacks, and I kinda… *allowed myself* to linger there for a bit, until she put her hands on my shoulders to put a couple inches between us. I gazed at her blue-green eyes, probably for a bit too long, smiled and took a breath.

"What are you doing here?" she asked, still wide-eyed.

"Ain't it obvious? I'm here to get you away from your ah… your—."

"Husband?"

"Yeah, that son of a bitch."

"Frank," she said, sounding irritated. I guess it was going to take a little while before she forgave me for taking off like a whipped dog when Roger finally caught up to her.

"Hey, sport," I said to Sam, tousling his hair. He made a face like a wince and backed away to fix his part.

The elevator came to a stop on the eleventh floor and a group of five younger men got on. Maggie, Sam and I scrunched up to the back to give them room. I tried to take Maggie's hand but she pulled it away. I stared at the back of the men's heads, then looked over at Maggie. Why wasn't she talking? What the hell was her problem?

I watched the subtle movements of the muscles in her face. She was tense, man. Like she was afraid of me. Then I stared down at her chest. Even though she was trying not to show it, I could tell she was breathing heavy by the way her breasts were heaving. I didn't know what to think of that, but I was a little disappointed that the boy wasn't a little more excited to see me. Here I was, there for the rescue, trying to be a hero to the kid, and he didn't seem to care one bit. I don't know. I guess I was thinking the kid and I had made some kinda connection. But, I guess, what it really was, was me just being some guy he and his mom camped out with for a few days. I was just some… just some guy.

"You really shouldn't be here, Frank," she whispered, finally saying something.

"I stuck an unlit cigarette in my mouth. "Yeah, why's that? You think I can't handle a guy like Roger? I know he scares you an awful lot, Mags, but to me he's just small potatoes."

"Was the guy who did that to your face small potatoes, too?"

I chuckled, realizing what I must look like to her. "Maggie, if the guy who did this was small potatoes, I wouldn't look like this."

She looked at me without a reply.

I sniffed, adjusted my belt buckle. "Matter of fact, he was a Green Beret… or some shit like that. Private detective. A real tough bastard."

"Private detective?" she said, keeping her voice low so the other guys wouldn't eaves drop. Not that it mattered to me. "Are you talking about Art Blansky?"

I hesitated. "Yeah, it was something like that, I think."

The elevator stopped again and one more person got on. A short man in a blue track suit. Blonde hair with a bald patch.

Maggie pressed in close, reached up to whisper in my ear. "Frank, Art Blansky called the room just a few minutes ago. He told Roger he was on his way over here. He said you would probably show up looking for me."

I felt the heat of her breath on the nape of my neck, the moisture against my ear lobe and felt myself becoming aroused. Even in an elevator filled with dudes my dick was getting hard. I wrapped my cast arm around her waist and pulled her close, put my lips on her neck and grasped her left tit with my good hand, felt it give under my gentle pressure.

My head rocked back and I felt a sting on my cheek.

"What do you think you're doing" she asked, still trying to be quiet. One of the guys looked back, but not for any reason other than curiosity, then turned back to stare at the door. Finally, we hit the lobby and everyone got out, except the short man in the track suit.

Maggie took Sam's hand and walked almost a little too quickly for me to keep up.

"I'm sorry about that, Maggie. I- I didn't mean anything by- by it."

She stopped and turned toward me. "You really don't want to be here, Frank," she said.

"Why the hell do you keep saying that to me?" I asked. "I'm here aren't I? If I didn't want to be here, would I be here? I'm telling you, I already took care of Art Blansky, and to hell with Roger and his... one hand."

Maggie's eyes softened and her head tilted to the side. "I know you mean well, Frank. And I know I'm the one who started this whole thing and got you involved, but Roger and I are going to work it out. For real this time." She smiled, sort of embarrassed. "I guess now he knows how far I'm willing to go." She looked down at Sam... who seemed to be off in a world of his own... even without the damn video game. "And he needs to be with his father. The only one he's ever going to have."

I squeezed my elbow above the cast. I was feeling that pressure again. I guess the bathroom attendant's medicine was wearing off. "It ain't no way to live, Mags," I said, kinda wanting to bash her in the skull. And I guess I *was* thinking about it.

You see, there's always going to be people like Maggie. That's what I figure. And so now, we have to come to some kind of conclusion. Do people like Maggie exist because of people like Roger, or do people like Roger exist because of cunts like Maggie? You know, the women that like to bring out the worst in men. Doesn't matter how sweet they look. How nice they act. It was like that with me and Maggie's sister, I think. She just brought out the worst in me. Of course, lucky for me, the worst in me isn't some Dr. Jekyll, Mr. Hyde thing. It's not violence. It ain't anything like that. It's a sort of... weakness. Like a... like all my will power just goes away. And I become a s-sniveling idiot. The first time she wanted out, I cried and begged. And the next time I begged

175

and yelled. And I just... become a person I don't want to be. You know what I mean?

"I'm really sorry, Frank," she said, looking like she meant it. "I'm sorry I made a mess out of your life for a few days. But it's not going to do anyone any good if you don't understand."

I took another long breath. "Let me get this straight," I said. "You came into my life, without me asking, and asked for my help... and now, here I am trying to help, and you don't want it."

She blushed, nodded.

"Ain't that some shit?" I said as a kind of statement, and I noticed she instinctively covered Sam's ears. And I thought, that's the secret, man. That instinct. Even if Maggie did like me, and even if I could rescue her and Sam from her abusive husband, I would never have that instinct. But I guess... I guess I didn't really care about rescuing them. I just wanted to be a hero by doing it. Seemed like a good way to step into something like that. And I guess... I guess I just wanted to fuck her, too. But there ain't nothing wrong with that. I figure a guy can do both things at once. At least that's what the funny books say.

I brushed my hand through my hair, felt it stick from all the grease. I hadn't showered for days. "Okay, Mags. I guess that's it, then. I'll be on my way." I shrugged. I wasn't going to fight it.

"I'm really sorry," she said again, and from the look on her face, I could tell she'd said it about enough times to not really mean it anymore. Kinda like when you tell a co-worker you're sorry when you hear their grandmother died. It's just plain politeness.

"I was just taking Sam to get a burger. We better get going or Roger will think I've run away again," she said with a smile and a fake, nervous laugh. And I didn't say anything, just sneered, and wondered if she realized that statement was a window by which to gaze at her future. She gave a self-conscious wave and turned, leading Sam out of the lobby and out to the streets. I didn't stare after her too long.

Well, Kimosabe, I believe the measure of a man's success is not just in the decisions he's made, but in the road he took to make them. And I guess I hadn't been too successful in playing the hero, but not for lack of trying or the justness of the cause… it was the road I'd taken. I just took the wrong road. But now I had a pretty good idea of how to get back on the right track. You see, I think I've always known I was going to commit the ultimate sin sooner or later, I was just waiting on a guy like Roger the half-hand to commit it against. I got turned back toward the elevator, pushed the button, and put myself on the right road.

# CHAPTER 14

I SLUMPED AGAINST the wall, between the bed and the bed table. My hands were slick and sticky from all the blood as I covered my stomach, and I kept trying to figure out when exactly I was going to stop bleeding.

Roger paced the floor on the other side of the room. I could see his reflection in the mirror behind the television. His face was in shadow. I watched him, almost as if that image was all he was, framed inside the mirror, like a moving picture on a screen, wishing I could just shut him off. But ol' Roger was shutting me off. I groaned, tasted blood in my mouth and closed my eyes.

Back before my dad became the way he did, he used to say to me, 'If you don't make yourself do some right, you're gonna start doing some wrong.'

I remembered the words but, luckily, just like Roger, his face was in shadow, too.

I had the elevator to myself the whole way up. I remember feeling strange. Lonely. A kind of lonely I hadn't felt before. Not a sad loneliness, it was more like a… like an *intermission*. All my senses were numbed. I could see, but I couldn't see. I could hear, but I couldn't hear. My body saw and heard, but my mind rejected the information. It was like I was on standby. Even my arm wasn't bothering me. I wasn't even thinking about what I was going to do to Roger.

I just knew. I knew how fast I was going to walk toward his room. I knew how hard I was going to knock on the door. I knew how long I was willing to wait between knocks. And I knew I was going to shoot him in the face as soon as he answered. You can't really call it a plan, but however you call it, it pretty much went that way, except I left the .38 in the Pontiac. Somewhere in the back of my head, I knew I couldn't bring a firearm onto the property.

Roger didn't waste any time. Before he'd opened the door all the way he got that steak knife about halfway inside me. I remember gasping, and grabbing his wrist just before the handle hit my belly button, but all it did was jerk the knife. He sawed at me for a second before grabbing my collar to force me into the room. He slammed the door shut as I sprawled over the mattress to land between the bed and the window.

There was like, lightening in my eyes, and I tried to sit up for some reason when Roger walked over to pick up the telephone by the bed. He dialed a number real slowly and looked away and began to speak. There was a fuzz in my head... like an insect's buzzing, so I couldn't hear what he was saying, but when he was finished, he put the phone back down on the receiver and walked over to pace in front of the mirror.

My breaths came in small little gasps to keep from extending my belly. This was done subconsciously, I never would have been able to think it. In fact, it was the little things like that that occupied my attention now. All the subtle things my body was doing without me. It was like... I'd screwed it up, and now it had to work without me. I kept putting a little weight on my hands, as if I was trying to lift myself up, but then I wouldn't move... as if I wasn't really trying to move. One of my legs kept trying to crawl under the other one. My head was leaning from left to right, back and forth, back and forth. I'd really made a mess of it. Man, I mean it.

I didn't even cover the gash, to put pressure on it until Blansky showed up.

There was a knock at the door and Roger's reflection rushed out of the mirror. I heard two voices and then nothing. And then Blansky stepped into the mirror. He looked down at me, one half of his face the color purple mixed with black. "Round two, mother fucker," he said with lips that could barely open.

I smiled.

The blood on my hands was acting almost like a glue, sticking them together, and Blansky gave my feet a kick. "Don't bother," he said. "That ain't gonna buy you but an hour or so." He turned to Roger, who I couldn't see, and asked, "How bad did you get him? Can he move?"

"You tell me, you're the expert," came Roger's headless reply.

Blansky kneeled down next to me and moved my hands out of the way. The monster that had become his face nodded. "It ain't as bad as it looks. Might be going into shock is my guess. Where's the blade?"

He stood back up and walked back to the mirror, so did Roger. Roger handed him the knife and Blansky laughed. "I knew you had it in you, Rog. But I expected you to wait."

"Get him the hell out of here," Roger replied.

Blansky pulled a plastic bag from his pocket and fit the knife into it. He wrapped the ends of the bag up and placed it on the dresser next to the television. "I can put him in a hole where he won't be found, but we still gotta get him out of the hotel. I got just the thing in the car. Hold tight, I'll be right back."

"What do you mean, hold tight?" Roger asked, grabbing his arm.

Blansky smiled out of half his mouth. "Well, we gotta dress the wound, keep him from bleeding out all over everything. And then I'm gonna pump his ass full of speed to get him mobile"

"Whatever you have to do," Roger said, sounding desperate. "Just make it quick. My wife and son will be back in another half hour."

"If they come back," Blansky chuckled, walked out of the mirror.

I heard the door open and shut, and Roger began to pace again. "Asshole," he snarled.

As soon as Blansky was gone, my body let out an involuntary groan. And I realized, what it was… was my ego testing the limitation of my body. There was a spasm of pain, but I found myself creeping back in, little by little, with it; and then the pain began to subside, like a shadow when the clouds come. I set my foot under me, and put some pressure on it, lifted my hip off the floor. I dragged my heel to meet with the back of my thigh, latched onto the side of the bed and managed to hoist myself up a healthy amount.

Roger never did notice me get to my feet, he was too busy staring at the carpet he was burning a hole in. And as I looked at the real Roger, not just his reflection, I got to thinking; you can never be quite the man you want to be. I doubt Roger wanted to be where he was at the moment. But me... I got to thinking about how just about everything I ever done was motivated more by hate than anything else. Maybe I didn't love quite as often as I should have. Maybe I didn't treat people quite as good as I should have. Little things I should have said and done...

Roger's scream like to burst an eardrum.

I'd chopped the steak knife down so hard it ripped through the plastic bag and severed the fingers he had left. He held his hand in front of his face, gushing blood all over himself. I left the steak knife next to the detached stubs and turned toward the door. Roger tried clawing at me but all he was doing was slipping and slapping his bloody palms down my back, on account of his not having any fingers left to grab with. But I was still a little weak, and he managed to put me down by throwing his whole body into mine. I hit the back of my head on the bed post and kicked him off me somehow. I tried to stand up again but it was beyond me. Roger was down by my legs, trying to crawl up to get at me. I was more concerned about being covered with his blood than with him personally. I lifted my leg, thinking to kick him away, but instead brought the heel of my boot down on his face. He made a strange *clicking* sound in his mouth, and then I shoved his face down toward his shoulders.

By the time Blansky came back, Roger's face was… not Roger's face. It was looking more and more like that shadowy reflection of his I'd seen.

Blansky shut the door and froze in his tracks. For the first time since I'd known him, he looked like a deer caught in the headlights. Ever since Roger stopped screaming, there was an intense quiet, and all I could hear was the blood pumping to my brain, like I was underwater. But I could hear Blansky sucking in air. I knew he was thinking about his choices. And I'll admit, I had put some limitations on that. But, still.

"I guess I'll leave it up to you, Frank," he said, a slight tremor in his voice.

I didn't say anything.

He stepped over to the dresser and looked down at Roger's fingers and the steak knife. He pulled another bag from his pocket, put the knife and the old bag in that one, rolled it up and put it in his inside pocket. He stared at his own reflection in the mirror for a bit before coming over to stand next to where I lay.

"What do you say, Frank? Can you speak?"

I didn't.

He bent down and took another look at my wound, pulled a roll of bandages and a needle full of something from his front coat pocket and dropped them on my lap.

"Now look at ya. You just gone and made it worse. You might've had a chance if you'd stayed put. But, now," he stood up and slapped his hands together, as if he were washing himself of me.

He put his hands on his hips, looked down at Roger, and then took in the whole of the suite, took a cigarette from the same pocket he'd had the bandages in, stuck it between his teeth and lit it. He stood there for a while... or, at least it seemed that way, sucked in the smoke, snorted, and said, "Adios, Frank."

And then I just... turned off, man.

And now the stage is bare, and I'm standing here, with emptiness all around. There it is. And here I am. The bleeding never did stop, but it's flowing more and more slowly, so, yeah, I guess that's a good sign. I walked as far as I could away from the hole I'd found myself in, until my legs wouldn't take me anywhere else. I ain't feelin' no pain, but it's not so bad. The sun will be here soon enough. You know, normally, a man won't last too long out here in the heat of the day, all alone with nothing but the elements, and the sun blazing down on them. But I figure there's been people who done it. Hell, the Indians did it for centuries. I figure I can too. There's a loneliness in it, that's all. But that's... that's the kind of thing I think I've gotten good at, no matter how much I tried to fight against it, or deny it to myself.

They say the mind can't tell time and death might not be real. I sometimes wonder, though... I sometimes wonder, if a man can fall asleep right at the end, and if he can dream, how long can he live the dream? Maybe forever. Maybe that's what life is all about; learning to live the dream. Learning to open up your mind so that it won't be nothing but black. But who knows, man? I guess I don't know too much, myself, and I've told you just about everything I do know. Most of the shit's true, too.

Whatever else, man, I think I'll be happy if I can just reach that dream. Remember what I said before, it ain't just the actions, it's the road you take. I guess when the sun comes out I'll try to find a better one. I ain't worried. The sun will come up to warm me. I can see it already with the way the sky is turning. That midnight blue is turning royal, getting richer, lighter and lighter. The stars are going out one by one. And it's… it's really something special now that I think about it. Now that I really look at it, it's the first great act.

Here it comes, man.